BERNARDO COUTO CASTILLO

A S P H O D E L S

TRANSLATED AND WITH AN INTRODUCTION BY
JESSICA SEQUEIRA

THIS IS A SNUGGLY BOOK

ISBN: 978-1-64525-050-0

BERNARDO COUTO CASTILLO (1879-1901) was born in Mexico City, to a wealthy family. After leaving school at the age of fourteen, he started to contribute to newspapers and magazines, and plunged himself into literary and artistic life. In the meantime, he worked as a clerk at the Treasury of the Ministry of Finance. He published his first story in *El Partido Liberal*; later fiction would appear in *El Nacional, El Mundo* and *La Revista Azul*. He was also a founder of the *Revista Moderna*, a pioneering magazine in literary *modernismo*. Couto Castillo lived for two years in Paris, and visited Germany and Switzerland. At the age of twenty-one, he died of pneumonia, a complication of addictions to alcohol and bromine. *Asphodels*, the only book to appear in his lifetime, was published in 1897.

JESSICA SEQUEIRA was born in San Jose, California in 1989, and currently lives in Santiago de Chile. Her works include the novel *A Furious Oyster* (Dostoyevsky Wannabe), and the collection of essays *Other Paradises: Poetic Approaches to Thinking in a Technological Age* (Zero). Her translations include Adolfo Couve's *When I Think of My Missing Head* (Snuggly) and Liliana Colanzi's *Our Dead World* (Dalkey Archive).

SNUGGLY BOOKS

CONTENTS

INTRODUCTION:
FLOWERS OF THE UNDERWORLD

IN Greek mythology, the asphodel is a
flower associated with death, and the
souls of ordinary mortals are sent to the
Asphodel Meadows, vast fields of the under-
world. In the twelve stories of *Asphodels*, the
Mexican author Bernardo Couto Castillo
(1879-1901), a cult figure due to his short
life and French-influenced decadent writings,
explores death in its many varieties, from the
wandering of Lady Death through city streets
in a merciless search for her next victim, to
the madness of a hypochondriac, to a murder
committed by an ultra-refined killer attracted
to the beauty of its "symphony in White and
Red", to the extraordinary final metaphysical
account of the torture of a soul. Although as-

phodels do not make a single appearance in the collection, they are like death: invisible, everywhere. The book itself is a field of asphodels, a gathering of first-person accounts that bloom as a witness to passing spirits. As the epigraph proclaims: "Death, she alone truly exists!"

Why are we are drawn to writers like Couto Castillo? They lure us with their intensity, their elegance mingled with deadly unpredictability, their erudite langour mingled with the sensual, perfectly encapsulated in the famous photo of the writer with a little mustache and a black cat rubbing against him, a frisson of fur against skin more immediate and comprehensible than any abstraction of love. We read Couto Castillo because as moderns we wish to be refined yet not bourgeois; delicate, precise, sophisticated and subtle, with a capacity to feel the most sublime nuances of sensation, yet without dissolving into a bland sentimentality. We read Couto Castillo because his exquisite writing, carved with greater care than a Jaipur dowry box, delights us with its novel and clever situations, yet has an iron core of anguish. Couto Castillo believed in cultivation—the cultivation of emotional states and the ability to produce and describe them with individual flair, as well as the cultivation of oneself as a reader, the faculty to find pleasure in unexpected characters and situations. This cultivation of pleasure is what he teaches the reader. Our complacent satisfaction with such an idea is stirred only when we remember how young he was when he died.

The ur-myth surrounding Couto Castillo, which haloes his reputation, is that he was an adolescent consumed by literary passion, devoured, cannibalized or eaten alive by his beliefs in excesses, diseases, artificial paradises, brothels and lyrical profusions at the expense of thought; that he was a creator of monologuing characters that speak of perverse feelings and tedium within society, cruel yet aesthetic urges, morality-free strangulations and knifings no legal court could have the good taste to understand; that he portrayed madnesses and beautiful self-inflicted pains with the greatest delicacy; and that he was a passive and willing victim, a Mexican successor to Baudelaire and Huysmans, in the imperialism no one ever talks about: the imperialism of the *poète maudit* legend. Couto Castillo's contemporary, José Juan Tablada, noted the young writer's affinity for this line of thought, calling him "a pale crewman on the sinister Ghost

Ship of Ennui". According to the canon of the French underbelly, which imposed its taste on Mexican bohemia, the height of elegance is to destroy oneself and leave behind just one slim volume, an embrace of eternal promise rather than a *longue durée* fizzle, in the ultimate performance of art for art's sake. Thus, so they say, did the work of the *enfant terrible* turn most terribly upon its creator.

But is this what truly happened? Let us look at the biographical facts. Bernardo Couto Castillo was born in 1879 into a wealthy family. He was the grandson of José Bernardo Couto Pérez, a well-known lawyer, senator, member of the Academia de la Lengua, director of the Academia de San Carlos and author, with a book called *Discourse on the History of Painting in Mexico*. The younger Couto Castillo studied at the Colegio Francés, which he left when he was fourteen. Determined to make his writings known at this precocious age, he visited newspaper and magazine offices in the company of his servant, and developed a reputation as something of a dandy. In 1893 he published his first story in *El Partido Liberal*; later stories, translations and articles would appear in *El Nacional*, *El Mundo* and *La Revista Azul*. Older writers welcomed him into their fold, and he became a familiar presence in literary bars and editorial offices. In the meantime, he worked as a clerk at the Treasury of the Ministry of Finance. Between 1894 and 1896 he made a trip to Europe, and during this time he lived in Paris, where he met Edmond de Goncourt; he also visited Germany and Switzerland. In 1901 he died of pneumonia, a complication of his addictions to alcohol and bromine.

Asphodels, Couto Castillo's only book, was published in 1897. He also wrote around twenty other texts for different publications, grouped as "Sunday Stories", "Dark Stories", "Mosaics", "Mad Stories" and "Fantastic Insomnias". He was a founder of the *Revista Moderna*, for which he edited the first issue before handing over the publication to Jesús E. Valenzuela. The twelve texts of *Asphodels*, however, remain the primary reference and point of entry into his corpus. According to Vicente Quirate, this work is "perhaps the most important manifesto by writers at the end of the nineteenth century, who made decadence their immediate banner and through their explorations of the body gave a scandalous send-off to the century they at once praised and condemned".

Could the myth also be a myth? How much water does the tale of Couto Castillo's self-destructive bohemianism hold? Behind the work of the most enduring of the *poètes maudits*, despite the glorification of drugs, madness, crime, violence, loose women and a bohemia outside of society, is the enigma of their ultimate attraction—to rigor. They were obsessed with structure, scholarship and intentionality of creation, and they carried out knowledgeable experiments with perspective and genre. This fascination with aesthetic forms, precisely the opposite of a chaotic launching of oneself into the abyss, may illusorily appear the same as self-destruction, only because the seduction of art leads these writers to give ultimate shape and melodrama to life itself.

Decadence is not just about pointing to the ill, the gangrene, the soulless elements of an increasingly industrialized society, but about finding alternative spaces, other paradises in which the norm need not reign. Disillusioned with society, decadent writers sought an alternative, but this could take many forms. One might find a buttress in Catholicism as Huysmans did, or like Baudelaire turn from opium and city strolls to the music of Wagner; Couto Castillo's exploration of thwarted lives temporarily led him to study classical works of French tragedy, which tend to attack the hypocrisy of society and extol the genuine man unafraid of voicing his individual opinions.

The formal culmination of a life need not arrive through suicide, as it did for *poètes maudits* such as Lautréamont, but might rather come through the discovery of the self and through aesthetic transfiguration. If these sound like quasi-romantic ideas, it is worth reiterating that romanticism is the other side of the decadent coin. It is notable that Couto Castillo did not deliberately kill himself. His death from pneumonia was an accident. He did not die by his own hand; he did not even go to meet death halfway. Everything in his papers suggests plans for a long life in literature. One can imagine him growing older and eventually constructing a literary masterpiece, not necessarily about himself, but full of further imagined protagonists who discover unique slivers of sensation and uncanny angles from which to evaluate a moribund civilization. It was society that was dying; the characters and the author were vibrant with life.

Couto Castillo believed in and was obsessed by death so much that he had no desire to seek it out. It would find him when it needed; in the meantime, he planned to work. He met with bad luck. But his circle on *La Revista Moderna*—Ciro B. Ceballos, Alberto Leduc, Balbino Dávalos, Jesús Urueta, Rubén M. Campos and Jesús E. Valenzuela—for the most part did just this, settling into prolific and long-lived careers in journalism and publishing.

Asphodels was written during the second government of Porfirio Díaz (1884–1911), when industrial advances at the turn of the century were accompanied by a widening disparity between the rich and the poor, and the fissures created by modernity were starting to grow more obvious. A *costumbrista* literature sprang up to describe the sweeping external changes, but complementary to it was the more internal literature of Couto Castillo and his circle, focused on the mind and emotions, exploring in particular the diseased and perverse imaginations of those who did not fit into society. This sense of alienation had its source not only in economic or educational disparities (many of Couto Castillo's protagonists are cultured aristocratic figures), but also in their questioning of the technological progressivism and bland rhetoric of utilitarian reasoning that so dominated the age in which they lived.

The court of law is an institution that seems to have particularly fascinated Couto Castillo; legal defenses, or the structured confession, appear in several stories in an almost parodic mode, with one talking head arguing against another in a machinery of justice that might as well cede a man his claim as condemn him to death, based on the words others speak. Reason comes to seem a shaky, fragile and untrustworthy scaffolding for the tell-tale, throbbing anguish of criminals, who in these stories are far from cool-headed. Writing long letters later buried in drawers, announcing their feats to an audience rather than retaining prudent silence, or mounting a totally invalid defense on the basis of aesthetic bliss, the characters possess a different set of morals than any court would recognize, and think in terms other than right and wrong. The chamber of horror and enigma beyond all explanation is not the chamber of law, but the human heart.

Along with its admirers, *Asphodels* has accumulated critiques and new readings with the passage of time. The women in Couto Castillo's work have been described as objects rather than subjects, pale and blonde in a French style very unlike that of the typical Mexican female. Couto Castillo's use of the violent imagination, such as his fantasies of killing women, girls and newborn babies, have also led some to question such strategies of shock, even as they admire his prose style. In Latin American literature, the "feminicide romance", in which a man kills his beloved out of jealousy and then recounts the tragedy in the form of a song or story, is a genre in itself. Couto Castillo's stories can additionally be put into the context of the *crónica roja*, a popular feature in Mexican newspapers from the nineteenth century to the present day, focusing on graphic descriptions of physical violence meant to titillate readers. Just as in these categories of "pulp", for Couto Castillo's characters, the inability to love properly can result in criminal actions or suicide, and are linked with troubling explanations of motive. In particular, many of these stories associate the inability to love properly—which can either result in suicide when turned against one's self, or the criminal act when turned against others—with factors related to family and culture.

With its critiques of society and its strong-voiced narrators in unusual psychological landscapes, *Asphodels* thus feels very contemporary. Troubling questions about how such supposedly morality-free tales powerfully condemn a culture obsessed with both violence and organization, and about how these portray individual subjectivity as it explodes from the stilted rhetoric of the bureaucratic state, accompany the reader through this dark classic of Mexican literature.

Yet ultimately, what grab tenacious hold of the mind are the words of the madman in the epigraph, full of awe and respect for the ultimate mystery, along with the personal anguish, rich psychologizing and artistry of these stories, timeless as Lady Death.

—Jessica Sequeira

SOURCES

Campos, Rubén M. *El bar. La vida literaria de México en 1900*. Universidad Nacional Autónoma de México, 2013.

Couto Castillo, Bernardo. *Asfódelos*. Mexico. Eduardo Dublán Impresor, 1897.

Couto Castillo, Bernardo. *Asfódelos*. Mexico. Instituto Nacional de Bellas Artes and Premià Editora, 1984.

Couto Castillo, Bernardo. *Cuentos completos*. Mexico. Factoría Ediciones, 2001.

Couto Castillo, Bernardo, ed. Coral Velázquez Alvarado. *Obra reunida, edición crítica, estudio introductorio, notas e índices*. Universidad Nacional Autónoma de México, 2014.

Gay, Juan Pascual. *El beso de la quimera. Una historia del decadentismo en México (1893–1898)*. El Colegio de San Luis, 2012.

ASPHODELS

. . . O Death! Sovereign Death, immensely pow-
erful, one and multiple, present, making her rule
felt at all hours in all places—Death, shadow
of God unfurling like an immense flag, lording
over the world, over beings and objects, surround-
ing everything, lying in wait for everything, clos-
ing it within a circle ever more narrow; Death,
she alone truly exists!

B. C. C.

ASPHODELS

THE JOY OF DEATH

for Jesús E. Valenzuela

OUR LADY DEATH felt profoundly bad-tempered. All night long she'd wandered from one side of the cemetery to the other, sweeping her white mantle along the avenues, cracking the bones of her hands and looking with her deep expressionless gaze at the white rows of tombs. She stopped before the sumptuous burial mounds, pursing her dry lips with a macabre gesture, and examined them with a great feeling of satisfaction, as she considered herself to be the owner of everything created, the sovereign shedder of tears, the terror of the poor world, the great one and All Powerful.

In the distance, a luminous cloud of dust rose up from the city; the bad-tempered one

23

watched it coldly, asking herself if everybody who lived there could fit into her gloomy domain. As she cast her gaze over the fields, she thought of replacing the wheat and trees with bare or engraved stones, and of putting out the city's shimmer with spadefuls of soil.

At dawn she began to move, thinking in silence. She was really quite displeased, to tell the truth, since no one from above helped her; times were poor to the point of excess, and for the whole year there had been no epidemic, no war, none of those massive bloodbaths that delighted her, filling her days with work and freeing her from gnawing tedium. To feed her worms, poor and weak creatures entrusted to her care, and to nourish the ravenous earth, she had to go from one place to another, plotting her approach, laying siege, putting a revolver or poison in the hands of the weary, upsetting mothers, and seeing herself forced to muffle pleas and abruptly push away the arms that defended beloved lives.

In her irritation, she proposed to herself to work hard and populate an entire avenue of the cemetery that disgusted her on her nocturnal strolls, when she found it virgin of human remains.

She entered fiercely as Lady and Queen into the first house she laid eyes upon, finding herself with an old man, which filled her with spite and increased her criminal impatience and irritation. His white hair made her think of the snow and cold of cemeteries. Wrinkles, withered faces, reminded her of her own existence, old now as the world. She looked above all for young faces, strong bodies and beings who would be missed, those over whom tears would be spilled.

The old man felt something abnormal happening inside him; his head and limbs grew clumsy, his feet went cold, his vision blurred and an immense terror filled him; alarmed, he shouted for a doctor. Death, exasperated, strangled the cry, broke the thread that held him to life, and moved away without emotion.

"Decidedly," she said, as she left, "I am too good and for that same reason too stupid. To take away an old man who in a few months would have gone on his own, to free him from a life that was only a weight, a constant shudder, a ruin! . . . No, decidedly I have been too good, and it's necessary to avenge my blunder."

As she walked on, a house further along in which everything seemed to smile drew her attention. Some houses look just like friendly faces with their freshly painted railings, very pale curtains and morning-glory vines on which bouquets of flowers are pinned; these houses stop the passer-by to make her jealous. "Pretty nest," murmured the visitor, "but we'll see in an hour's time." Cracking the bones of her hands, she went straight to a bedroom in whose depths the bed appeared, raised up like a throne.

The wife was asleep. Death touched her naked arms, making her shiver from cold, then lightly pressed on her neck to ensure a little anxiety. She gave her time to call out, watching with pleasure how everyone grew alarmed, and laughed at the running around and the jars that were brought out. Then she prolonged her cold caresses and gave a deep bow, accompanied by a horrible grimace to the doctor as he came dashing in. She pressed down again, with more force, and moved her infected mouth close to inhale her victim's breath; she passed her rough fingers over the beautiful body and squeezed her heart. When she grew tired after having played with this life as a cat plays with a rat, she gave a hard shake and moved away impassively, smiling at the chorus of wails that followed. A long series of murders followed; wherever she felt like going, she left behind shuttered windows, houses where the abandoned looked at each other with shifting eyes without daring to speak a word, and long litanies of prayers interrupted by sobbing. At four in the afternoon, somewhat tortured by so much crying, she went to the bedroom of one who was calling her.

There she was received as a Redeemer; the cold fingers, long and hard as pincers, seemed gentle and soft; the worn face and hideous gesture took on a young merciful form and arrived as a beloved to imprint the sacred kiss; the damp mantle and half-tattered shroud seemed light chiffon covering a body dreamed of for many nights and desired through all the swooning hours.

The blessings she received there disgusted her once more, and as she looked around for another person to bring with her, she stumbled across a doctor.

"Ah! Señor Doctor, off you go in such a hurry! No doubt to snatch some pensioner away from me. Your science is so great, you bestow so much health and life, that I, poor death, am in need of you." After saying this she roughly handled the learned man, so busy with the deaths of others he hardly took any care with his own: in haste he went to a chemist's and asked for water and powders, but just as he was preparing to drink them, the irritated mistress of the cemetery finished him off with a sharp slap.

At night, before she returned to her domain, some brilliant lights attracted her attention; slowly, she went into a circus. Like a good tyrant, the pleasure of others offended and disturbed her, making her feel that she was being deprived of something. The lights, the vibrant colors, the orchestra stoked her rage; but it consoled her to think that all of them there, absolutely all of them, belonged to her, the joyful as much as the fed up, the intelligent as much as the stupid, the powerful as much as the wretched. All of them were flesh that would fatten her worms; by merely stretching out her hand or blowing with strength, she could interrupt the laughter and thwart the applause, and nobody, absolutely nobody, would be able to free themselves from her yoke. "Goodbye, then, young faces, beautiful faces, inflamed hearts and beings in hope of fortune; none of you believe you are mine; you think, you move, you make noise and your vanity swells up straight away, making you imagine you are free and the owners of yourselves, ah!

"Ah! Poor madmen! I alone control you; you have belonged to me from the start of the centuries and will belong to me until my bones break under the ruins of the Universe. Laugh, laugh, make the movements that bring me horror; the thread of your life, poor puppets, is in my hands. Laugh, act out your comedy until the string breaks and you fall on the cold floorboards, the mournful stage of silent tragedy that will be your coffin."

Her threatening monologue was interrupted by the appearance of a clown, white as she was. He made ironic gestures to parody the pain of unreciprocated passion; on his wide silk suit, he flaunted immense skulls, delicately embroidered, crying through empty orbits. "Hello!" exclaimed the gloomy observer, "Hello! You are playing with me and mocking my pain, my little friend; I will suppress your laughter, so you never laugh again because of your own pain." Immediately she left for the clown's house.

"Baby", the boy who cheered up this home with the sound of his laughter and the constant movement of his little body, was resting from his ceaseless running about and endless chatter. The gleam of a blue lamp fell onto his face. Baby smiled as he slept, with his tiny fists clenched and an air of satisfaction.

The criminal stopped for a moment; although she didn't like to confess it, she felt weakness, something like regret over tearing away such a beautiful angel and swapping out his never-still features for unchanging lines, changing his constant bustle for the most absolute silence. She thought of the kisses and caresses he must receive every day, of the deep laughter he could draw from his not always joyful father, of the care that surrounded the boy, and she almost drew back. But her weakness stopped her; she raised a finger to her temple and looked again at the child. "Come now," she said, "am I really going to turn compassionate? No, my honor will not allow it." And the work began.

What appeared simple did not turn out to be so. The mother shielded the child, defended him, protected him and used her body to cover him to avoid the embraces of the cruel one.

When she felt his little limbs freezing, she gave them her own heat, and when his breathing grew difficult, she gave him her breath.

Those were anxious hours. Sometimes the frozen fingers would touch the delicate flesh, but the mother would rub the child to make his blood circulate. Life slowly returned, the small eyes opened and the pale head framed in blond hair recovered, until a few minutes later the fingers touched him again, and the cold came back, and the paleness was greater.

The struggle lasted several hours, with the mother never tiring, and Death grew furious. There was a moment she thought of taking the defender as well, but then there would be no pain, and the triumph would be incomplete.

In the end she was victorious when the mother went away for just a moment, leaving the little body exposed.

The honor of Death, as stupid as the honor of men, had done away with Baby.

The next day her victims arrived, one by one. She received them ceremoniously, paid them respects, sped along the gravediggers, turned up the earth and set the bells ringing. The coffin of the married woman came covered in flowers full of freshness and life, an irony present at every funeral. The boy came in his little box, white and cushioned like a bed. The old man and the young man and others came too, placed at a short distance from one another on the avenue that the previous day had been deserted, and was now full of flowers. The heartbroken came, faces grief-stricken and sincere, faces indifferent and idiotic, faces put on for the occasion like the special suits worn, like the words spoken.

The boxes disappeared, the flowers suffocated under spadefuls of earth, the tears dried up and once again there was only silence.

That night the moon shone in all its splendor. Near the cemetery the dogs barked; in the distance, the city displayed its thousands of luminous points, glittering like stars in the dark sky; wind swayed the branches that gave shadow to those beds which never felt heat. Death strolled past the tombs; she opened the ones that had just been covered, rejoicing to see that the pure young body of the wife, which a day before had been sleeping in loving arms, now appeared yellow with bluish patches, food for the worms. She encouraged them in their work, after carefully observing the places where they most liked to gather; she went to the boy, mussed the hair that fell over his wax-colored face, and squeezed the little hands that used to move everything about; she shook the bodies, intoxicating herself with their smells; then she moved away with indifference, hounded once again by a vast sense of tedium.

But her great satisfaction, her deepest pleasure, was to think that just as all of them belonged to her now in body, they would belong to her completely in a month, a year or two years, when oblivion had erased them from the memory of mankind. Death moved away; it had not been an entirely bad day.

AN OBSESSION

for Jesús Urueta

IN a small Louis XV dresser I recently bought, I found the following letter at the bottom of a drawer:

Dear friend,

What I write to you is going to come as a great surprise; but you have no idea the state of excitement and thought in which I find myself. You, my greatest companion in other times, the one who knew all my joys and anxieties, you are the only one who can hear me out and console me in my desolation. Come, come live by my side and be my companion as in days past; only now I will not laugh, or be the rowdy devil from back then . . . Come my friend, since I am afraid for my poor reason, which is already deeply shaken!

You must remember that a short time after you left the life of commotion and disorder we had carried out together for so long, to wisely shut yourself away in a retreat of peace and work, I wrote to you saying:

"Friend, at last I have found what I needed: the submissive and calm creature by whose side I can take refuge, the being made for love, tolerant of my whims, humble toward my desires, who starting today will be my partner."

I spoke to you of her, of her gentle face, of her serene and welcoming gaze, of her locks parted in the middle of her forehead that fell straight over her temples, like those of a Pre-Raphaelite virgin. I presented you with the case of conscience in which I found myself, for she was an honest creature and duty demanded that I give her my name, while my convictions, or to put it better, my stupid preoccupations, opposed themselves to any official and definitive link. I knew well that she desired nothing but to obey me; her mother, her home, everything was quickly sacrificed to my slightest desire; she would have gone to church or to the worst of the places chosen by me with the same pleasure, or rather, the same enthusiasm. In her poor existence as a woman I was the long-awaited one, the indisputable master, the invitation she was expecting before her swift surrender. With my usual egoism and neglect, I told myself: "There will be time later", and made her mine.

Her mother died, and I brought her to live with me without thinking of formalizing her status, interested only in the charm that radiated from her entire being.

You cannot imagine the two years of full and complete happiness I spent by her side. I had never believed in happiness, and had not thought that a man of some refinement could with no great effort put up with the same caresses, same features and same habits for two years. But just look: I, the very egotistical skeptic you knew, was happy by the side of a woman; happy as only a man can be who is fated to pay for it incredibly dearly, just as I am doing now. Every day that goes by, every hour that flits past, I regret those two years more bitterly and desire them with greater intensity; I have been wounded for eternity, and been left just like Adam after his expulsion from Paradise.

For the two years my passion lasted, I never even considered deceiving her; do not be astonished, for you did not know her; she never gave the same kiss twice, nor repeated the same caress; never did any vulgar phrase come from her small lips; she was capable of every seduction and every goodness; she was indulgent, and you know that the moment when the desire to deceive is greatest, when the appetite of the *demon of perversity* is whetted, is when the setbacks and poorly-timed jealousies appear. With her, even if at a given time these sprung up terribly as in every genuine lover, so long as she did not know, so long as no one ever showed up to trickle doubts into her consciousness, the idea that I could ever truly be false never passed through her mind; for her, I was all that was great and beautiful, just as for me, she was all that was precious.

Do you remember Charles X? To him, to him alone do I owe my tragedy; he was the black hand that hides in the shadows and delivers the mortal wound; he was the false friend created to strike like a viper, fatal and treacherous; he was the miserable Iago who entered my house to torment, poison and make night of our happiness. You know that I sought him out to provoke him into a duel, in which he even had the luck to wound me, he, whom I should have destroyed by the strength of my hate alone!

37

One day, when I arrived, I found Julia sobbing; you can imagine my astonishment when she answered my caresses only with reproaches. I wanted to know, I demanded it . . . and I found out. The wretched one! . . . he, who had sat at my table every day smiling, had spoken of me, of my past, of the women I had enjoyed and everything I had done; he had quoted dates, given proofs; he had added that my intention was to do the same with her, and that if I had not married, if up to that point I had denied her my name, it was to be able to abandon her without consequence, once I had tired of her. My poor adored creature shook with pain as she choked out this statement between tears.

In vain did I try to console her. After the tears came furious reproaches; within her awoke the anger of the woman who, trusting until then, feels herself to be totally deceived. I had not been what she believed, what she loved; then came the spite that wished to wound, to take revenge, and a new being revealed itself before me. The weak, submissive, kind-hearted one turned into an irate lioness that only wanted to lash out, to destroy. "You will marry me," she said, "I will not be like the others, no, you will not deceive me, oh no, not me! You will marry! You will marry!" and this cry bubbled up constantly from her rage, like foam from churning water.

In her enraged look there was resentment, there was scorn, and my pride, my stupid male pride rose up against the one I most loved, against the one I felt I loved even at that moment I did not recognize her. "Marry? And who can force me? Perhaps you, who have come for your own pleasure?"

A period of silence followed my words; I saw her astonishment at the way my fury rose up in turn against hers, with a strength matched against what she had thought was hers alone. Then, after a brief pause and a few directionless steps, she went to the night table beside her, seized a revolver and aimed it at me, crying out mechanically: "You will marry, you will marry, I . . ."

I laughed, making an effort to hurl barbs of irony at her, and pale, without speaking a word, she pressed the barrel against her forehead. She looked at me for a moment with a gaze I've never been able to forget, an indescribable gaze that pursues me in the shadow of night and torments me in bad dreams. In this gaze there was a determination, as well as reproaches, but the reproaches were still full of love . . . I didn't take a step, I didn't make a gesture, I didn't lift an arm to stop her; on the contrary, intrigued, with a perverse curiosity, I waited, and even seemed to defy her with my attitude.

An explosion, and I sprinted forward in time to catch her in my arms . . . a final convulsion, then nothing, a gush of blood covering her face, soaking everything!

Who could precisely describe and analyze everything I felt that night holding vigil over she whom I had so loved, she whom I felt more and more clearly I loved now that she had ceased to exist. I have only vague memories. Her body, the lines of her perfect body stood out against the black of the funeral tapestry spread on the bed beneath her. The whiteness of her hands, the cadaverous paleness of her face were brightly accentuated against the black, like ivory enamel. The wound on her forehead had been bandaged, and only a small red dot stained the silk that wrapped it; her loose hair served as a pillow. On her small lips that had once smiled so much, a nest of caresses, but were now cold and insensitive as marble, there had appeared a slight crease of pain. The closed eyelids separated me forever from her gaze. After that I don't remember anything else . . . Gusts of air entering to sway the light of the candles, sending yellow gleams over the face of the departed. The plaintive and ironically joyful notes of barrel organs, the flitting movements of flies and the chimes of passing hours echoing abruptly, heavily, inevitably in the silence of night, as well as many thoughts, a great deal of brooding in my mind over ideas and memories.

Once again I lived through the scenes and caresses of those two years; I saw her, I saw her unchanging, impassive, submerged in the depths of her dream of death; I took her cold hand, I called out to her, unable and unwilling to admit that she was dead. Dead, and for what? What had she done, what had we done? She remained impassive and the seriousness of her face spoke to me of all that separated us: she was so far away! I no longer existed for her! This disappearance, this thinking about the solitude of the next day and the finality of her death, made me desperate and furious at my helplessness as well as at the force that creates beings, only to destroy them with such ease.

I thought of my guilt, of my criminal pride. A movement, a word, a plea would have been enough for her to be alive, lavishing me with her caresses and murmuring loving words in my ear . . . then I saw her again . . . the same crease in her face, her eyes closed forever, candles casting luminous gleams over her body and tinting her long hair in bronze.

I repented, I hated myself, and all was in vain; no force, absolutely none at all would bring back the gentleness of her smile or the shine of her eyes. Days would follow days, and to wait for her would be in vain. Men would go on with the same acts, the same gestures, the same words; nothing and nobody would change, and she, she who ought to be fluttering and moving about like the others, would forever remain sunk beneath the earth: all because I had not spoken to her, had not stopped her. For me, constant desolation.

For her . . . ?

I saw her go out of the room and had no strength to accompany her; unknown hands shut her away in her new dwelling for eternity; the final words addressed to her came from lips that had never kissed her; I was left dazed and stunned as after great and definitive catastrophes.

Once resigned to the fact of her death, I began the long pilgrimage, the awful inspection of objects and trifles she had chosen and in whose familiarity I lived, beginning the long ordeal of reconstruction, detail by detail, of my prior happiness. Everything reminded me of her, I found her in everything, and everything was still full of her presence. The mirrors had not forgotten her image, her gloves had not lost the shape of her hands, there were pillows that still bore the hollow shaped by her head, and the stain, the fatal blackish-red stain, presented itself to me at every moment to resurrect the scene.

Not being able to resist all this, I left the house where together we had known so many joys and where I had spent such periods of bitterness alone. Then began long, wearisome days of continuous wandering and fleeing from her memory like an ingrate, days when I struggled not to go back to the reliquary where her memory is hidden and her image floats. I reached the house, looked at the closed doors and empty balconies that all proclaimed abandonment and death, and feeling myself weak, went and drank until I blunted my pain; but then the vision of her body as it fell into my hands, the expression, oh!, the expression of loving reproach that came from her eyes as she left life and the blood that covered her body came to torment me, appearing as the most horrible of nightmares.

After some time, I came back, resolved to work without rest. I spent many days and nights leaning over my table, nervously filling pages and pages, hoping for fatigue and fictional ideas to pull me away from my thoughts. Often the very words I was writing brushed against and reopened my wound, and often, forgetting for a moment, I would look for her again by my side, as I had done when she had accompanied me as I worked; when I didn't find her, I threw away my pen, and sank even deeper into my pain.

But here is where the darkest part begins, what the constant egoist in me worries about most in this drama. Do not laugh.

One night, after several hours of work, I heard a slight noise behind me; since I was quite nervous, I turned around abruptly. I needn't tell you that I didn't find anything. I went on working, now somewhat agitated and suspicious of the thick shadows beyond the glowing radius of my lamp; a short time after this I felt, or thought I felt, a light touch on my shoulder; I went cold, remembering how she used to let me know this way when she wanted to interrupt my work, and felt a horrible anxiety. I didn't dare turn my head, I almost didn't breathe, afraid there would be something behind me. After a period of struggle, at last I moved my head slowly, gasping from the effort . . . Nothing! Only half shadows and the gold gleam of the book bindings. I breathed deeply, with relief, but still scared, let my pen drop. Without turning around again, with icy forehead, I went straight to bed.

There's no need to tell you I couldn't sleep a moment; the slightest noise, the chiming of the hours, the creak of a piece of furniture, the passing of a rat, everything produced cold sweats and shocks in me, despite the level-headed reasoning I gave to it.

But since then, my friend, everything has been like this; everything startles me, and I always work with an alert ear, hoping to catch every noise by surprise. In a word, I am afraid, afraid of the poor suicide whom I loved so much. I am afraid she will return, afraid more than anything of the final look in her eyes, which I cannot and will not ever be able to forget. I am not mad, no, but I feel her wandering invisibly around me, and am afraid, afraid of her; in such a way that never and not for anything would I have dared to write this at night, afraid of feeling the tap on my shoulder or her cautious, silently advancing steps: I am afraid!

I am afraid, yes, and of her; come, come and free me from this dread, from this constant, unbearable anguish. With someone by my side, I will feel strong. I've thought of marrying, of bringing someone close to shield me from her, but no, I would feel her jealousy, and could never kiss or embrace my wife without feeling her between us, invisible.

It isn't that I've stopped loving her; no, I love her and desire her as never before, for my days would not be so dark with her by my side. But you understand. I loved her a lot, she loved me a lot, I was very happy, and now it is necessary that I pay with the worst of punishments: fearing her, wanting to protect myself against her.

You see! Even now, when writing to you, the plaintive sound of a door pushed by the wind (is it the wind?) . . . has made me shudder and turned my forehead to ice. Yet I do not dare turn my face.

I am afraid! I am afraid! Come my friend, come, or I don't know what will happen to me.

FINAL HOURS

THE yellow of the lamp on the night-stand, and the white of the clothing of the bed, were all that could be glimpsed at first in the vast room.

When your eyes grew used to this semi-darkness, you saw a skinny face with livid yellow tones in the bed, and damp anguished eyes anxiously fixed with all their remaining life on the bedroom door. Along with these were some long bony hands that dug into the sheets and waved around, flailing tarantulas that with mechanical and instinctive move-ments constantly pulled the covers toward the face, as if, in accordance with the theory of a famous contemporary psychologist, they already desired to cover themselves with the shroud.

At the door there appeared the silhouette of the doctor, a tall figure wrapped in a long frock coat; the eyes of the patient threw out sparks; the dignified steps of the dark figure went toward a rocking chair where a young, still beardless man yawned with boredom; then a few words were exchanged and the steps moved toward the bed, where the eyes dilated and a barely perceptible voice stammered:

"I will . . . will live . . . one year . . . two at most, Doctor."

The doctor gave no answer, but an involuntary expression of pity on his flawlessly stoic face made the ill man's restless hands jump and his skeletal body toss and turn.

The doctor stood without moving, looking at the forsaken one with the attitude of mingled compassion and curiosity felt by even the most accustomed when faced with travelers unwilling to cross the fatal line. The wretched one, reading his sentence in this look, made an effort to control himself and take courage, as in his head he soliloquized:

"Now! . . . Everything is over! . . . It had to happen . . . And what? . . . What is life? What will I leave, what will I long for, what could I miss after I am dead?" and in vain he tried to reconcile himself to the fact that he was old;

that he had neither son, nor brother, nor wife; that in his heart there was nothing, absolutely nothing, not even memories. Had he wanted something in this world beyond egoistic tranquility? No, isn't that right? Others carry on even through ruin, and at the moment of their death see faces traced out that smile or cry, passing figures of friends, memories of good periods fading away; while for him, there was nothing, nothing, nothing, the most complete emptiness, and yet . . .

Yet he clung to life, he clung eagerly, with all his will and strength, as if such strength were able to overcome death . . . and he looked back on what had been his life, the most common, the most lacking in events, the most monotonous of existences, able to drive even the most easily contented novelist to despair.

His childhood? A few years of shyness; he did not remember echoes of loud laughter, or sprints or tumbles; at that moment he did not hear childish shouts, or the chirping of mischievous birds that called out or pecked at him. In his youth, there had been two events: the death of his father, and almost immediately following it, the death of his mother; for him everything about these two facts could be represented by two nights spent beside the corpses, looking after the candles as they burned and gave off sparks, and afterward eating alone, with two places fewer at the common table. Apart from this, all was unchanged: there were the same maids, the same house, the same facts and the same words.

He saw mobs of young people going about laughing, to their ruin perhaps, but a ruin preceded by the clinking of glasses and the echo of laughter; he saw magnificent and smiling women, and the noisy declarations of twenty-year-olds, and he fled, afraid of expenses, of movement, of leaving his moldy old tortoise shell.

Never had he wanted to form a home, out of this same horror of expenses and arguments; the little blonde heads and pale dresses that surrounded tables and beds, and livened up sickrooms like talking flower bouquets, were for him nothing more than a certain number of mouths to feed, a quantity of dresses and teachers, an endless number of pesos that disappeared, siphoned off with incredible speed.

To deposit a certain sum of money, to change his housekeeper, were the sorrows of his life; his pleasures were to go to a public garden on a specific day of the week and do the same turns, hear the same strident tones of the brass band, find the same faces and admire the same common idylls.

Every now and then, to absolve his conscience, or rather, with the hope of being amply rewarded in another life, he put a few coins into one of those trembling, stiff, dirty hands held out in supplication to passers-by; now he recalled these actions at every moment. He was full of self-flattery, and would have been able to recount his actions even to God himself, repeating them, making Him jot them down in a book, nearly demanding an invoice; he would do this with great pleasure.

In his last years he somewhat regretted not having married, but only because in a woman he would perhaps have found an attentive nurse, someone whose care might have prolonged his days. As the doctor was still there, he said to him:

"Three years, Doctor, at most. I'll marry and my wife will take care of me. It's not true that . . ."

He made a gesture of horror, his hands jumped nervously, the sheets rose even further, and with a new gesture, his eyes took on the stillness of agate, the gaze of the dead.

51

"It's over!" said the physician, taking his pulse.

"At last!" exclaimed the beardless nephew inheriting his uncle's money, unable to contain his indiscreet happiness.

And this was the only funeral oration or speech the death of this good gentleman drew from any human mouth.

THE INEVITABLE

for Francisco M. de Olaguibel

HESITATING, he reached the door to the room; there he stopped to rest. What a climb and what a walk! With his hands he pressed down on his chest, wanting to hold back the thumping of his heart, at the same time as he took deep greedy breaths.

Then he passed his hand over his forehead, and when he felt it damp from sweat, his whole body shuddered. He looked at his hand, he stared at it for a long time with eyes of terror, and after shaking it, he rubbed it against the wall as if trying to get rid of something.

He felt an immense fatigue and an even more exhausting anguish. In his head incoherent ideas did turns, fragments of works or acts he couldn't specify; he wasn't aware of the hour, despite the fact that in his agitation he'd pulled out his watch over a hundred times.

He sat on a step, hid his head between his hands, and remained unmoving, without a thought, without any notion of things, in a state of perfect numbness.

In the distance a bell chimed. Below he heard voices and steps, and with a shudder, he stood up. His limbs all trembled, and attempting to make himself smaller, wanting to sink into the shadows, he held back a gasp.

Alongside him people passed, a lady, a girl, a few others. He didn't move, he didn't breathe, but his forehead sweated in terror. Oh! His heart, his heart beat with frenzy, making a horrible sound, echoing in his ears like hammer blows. How could these people not hear him?

Behind the door a vibrating voice stopped every movement of his blood. There were ideas in his head; he trembled for a moment, and on his lips a triumphant smile appeared. He felt like someone else; he put his hand into his pocket and sunk it in the gold he was carrying; he pulled out a fistful, looked at it, brought it to his lips and kissed it as one kisses a beloved. Tucking it away again, he knocked on the door.

When it opened a crack, he saw first a naked arm, perfectly shaped, an arm white as the fistful of lace from which it emerged, and then a beautiful face, severe, with inquiring eyes that stared at him at the same time as an irritable "not again" emerged from the lips.

"Listen," he said in a quavering voice, "the thing is that now . . . now I'm bringing you what you want, what you need . . . now I have money . . . a lot of money."

She looked at him from head to foot, examining him, trying with a look of doubt to penetrate to the depths of his pockets.

Understanding, feeling humiliated by this inspection, he raised his head and pulled out a handful of gold.

"Gold! Gold for you!" he cried, and went in.

A small bedroom like a niche adorned to excess, fragrant as a mosque, soft as a bed; divans and cushions everywhere to lull the idle body to sleep; and on a platform in the depths, a low and very charming bed, with lovers painted on the wood and long drapes to conceal it, in the style of a throne.

On a small table, cups and bottles with silver stoppers, a countless number of little objects, a thousand trifles made to distract the fickle gaze of the woman who possessed them.

Seated, with eyes fixed on the toes of her glossy feet, which played about like small lively mice over a bear skin, she listened without attention.

"What luck to have found you alone! And so you will be for many days, a very long time perhaps. Now that I am rich, I'm just like those who visit you whenever they like. I'll be your master, at least as much as they are; now my turn to possess you has come, even if only because of how much I've desired you; and it's been a great deal, oh! yes! a great deal and for a long time, do you remember? Ever since you drank a glass of champagne with me at the party given by . . . I was poor then, I'd been brought by a rich friend and could do nothing . . . but I could love you, and did love you. I loved you with all the deep strength of which I am capable; I loved you and loved you in all ways, with tenderness and fury and desire. You were the only thing that mattered, the purpose of my life. In the daytime I followed you through the streets, seeing only your slow walk, unhurried like a Queen's; I reached your door and saw you disappear, and your shadow on the balcony consoled me. I saw men enter, all known to me, all with money, and at night in my rooftop room, biting the pillow, I cried; yes, how I cried, with rage and impotence . . .

"I knew that not everything in you was bad, that there could be, that there was a sensitive place; I knew that you'd loved a man, a wretched one at whom I'd wanted to shout so many times when I saw him go into your house: 'Idiot, why do you let them snatch her away from you, steal her, share her amongst themselves; why don't you flee with her somewhere far, very far away, where no one can take her from you?' . . . I knew that you loved someone, and that he wasn't me!"

"My God! How excited you are," she said, and went on without stopping, "but now, now you're mine, mine at least as long as this gold lasts. After that . . ." and she made a vague gesture.

In the darkness of the narrow room, the only light came from a small lamp with irradiations of opal.

The best moments were over. Limp with caresses, fatigued with kisses, she closed her fickle eyes, overcome by heavy sleep. He stayed awake and looked at her small body covered in lace, her breasts and face that bloomed from it like a strange flower from complicated leaves; he looked at her with disturbed eyes that might have held gratification, or tenderness, or hate. Occasionally sparks of anger came from them; his eyelids were half-closed, as if they wanted to distance themselves from her, but his eyes insisted, breaking from their prison to fasten once again upon her, eager, lustful, desiring to stare at her forever.

He wanted to sleep but rest denied itself to him, just as she had denied herself to him before that night; he wanted to sleep, to forget himself in his happiness and no longer hear what turned over and over in his brain, no longer feel the flame burning inside him which he could not put out.

His gaze separated from her, and then from amidst the shadows, a thousand bizarre and nonsensical figures came toward him; all his past tortures, all his desires and

vain pleas; all the luminous nights spent fever-
ishly imagining another man who had been
consuming himself in her torture. In endless
procession, there passed all the evil thoughts
he had incubated, in the shadow of his idea of
her; all the unhealthy ideas, all the corruption
and lewdness that the image of this woman
seven times a sinner had provoked in his desire-
lashed brain.

The figures approached, surrounded him
and pressed in upon him. He felt the impulse
to shout; but a cry far greater than the strength
in his lungs, along with a constant clinking of
gold, stopped him.

She half-opened her eyes and looked at
him.

"You aren't asleep," she said.

"No, I don't know what's wrong with me. I
feel agitated, and how could I not be, finding
myself by your side?"

This strange flower, with a perfume more
venomous than any other, smiled; once again
she let her eyelids droop, their closed pet-
als resting in the unmoving position of an
opulent decorative plant. Sleep fell upon her,
dense as the shadows. He ran a hand through
his untidy hair.

"I was dreaming," he said, in an attempt to stay calm, but a small noise made him shiver. Listening for the tiniest sound, he remained on guard, alert.

The lamp shook a bit, and its opal rays trembled over the carpet and walls.

The obsessive procession of figures emerged once again. The bad thoughts, the dishonest ideas he had suffered, paraded before him; but now, at the end of them, black and reddish, was the most recent one, the latest. The crime.

A very cold sweat passed over his entire body . . . a cold identical to that of the other . . . of the dead man, the one he had strangled.

Having reached the limit of his desire, having in his head the fixed, obstinately fixed idea of this woman glimpsed at a party, sought out and loved in solitude for so many days and nights; having met with her rejection, his eyes had closed, and in his head there had been something like a flapping of wings. With unprecedented lucidity and extreme calm, he had conceived of the idea of killing if necessary, to acquire the gold that would open the door and the arms of his beloved.

He had an uncle, an old, rich and stingily greedy uncle, and his scheming had been directed toward him.

"What's the matter?" she said again. "You can't be calm for a moment."

"No, the darkness of this room bothers me." Light appeared as she lit a small glass lamp. She returned to her original position, and he, closing his eyes, tried to sleep . . .

A big, very big room, with a small bed next to a wardrobe, and lying down, a small thin old man dozing over a book.

He'd gone in the afternoon to visit him and talked about things he couldn't remember; he'd attempted to be pleasant and inspire confidence; he'd said goodbye and then instead of leaving he'd hidden himself away, anxiously waiting for nightfall.

Shadows surrounded the house, darkened the windows and closed in like curtains, extinguishing everything. The hours chimed slowly on a clock, and at a moment that no sound terrified him, he left his hiding place for the big room with the small bed, where he found the old man resting, still leaning over his book.

The scene was very short.

"What do you want?" stammered his uncle, when he saw him in the room, having appeared like a ghost. "Who let you in?"

"Nobody, and I want your money."

"My money! . . . My money for you! Are you perhaps mad?"

"I'm not mad and I want it; you have no need of it but I, I need it."

The old man laughed and the young man threw himself upon him, upon his neck.

"Keys!"

The old man didn't move and he pressed and pressed, threw him down on the bed, lifted his knee, put it on the victim's chest and kept pressing with all his strength, like a savage, until he tired; when he moved his hands away, the old man was dead.

He took the keys, opened the wardrobe and filled his pockets with bills, gold, valuables, letters, everything he found: he was in a fever of possession; his blood boiled, and his brain wanted to burst out with a leap from his skull.

How did he leave? How did he cross the streets to reach her? He didn't know, he remembered only that his legs had buckled and that he'd drunk many glasses of wine; and then . . .

Then had come the triumph, the complete realization of the desire toward which his entire being had aspired for so long. No more nights of angst spent in useless insomnia with his spirit harassed by the idea of this woman forbidden to him for reasons of poverty. He'd spent moments of absolute oblivion, when her two lips had half-opened, invited him and joined fragrantly with his trembling ones, when his hands had been able to clasp and play with her smaller versions, when her hair had shaken loose in streams of sweet-scented molten gold, when she had half-closed her eyes . . . he had forgotten everything then, his past anxieties, the scourge of his thoughts, his crime, everything! He was living for the present moment alone, savoring his fleeting current happiness with as much intensity as he had desired, and if at that moment she had asked for another death, without hesitation he would have strangled the first passer-by, should this mean that he could come see her again, and forget himself by her side.

Once the first moments had passed, back in the fatiguing calm of the boudoir, his thought exploded, putting him face to face with himself, abruptly confronting him with his action. It was a confused mix of fears and reproaches: the next day, tomorrow, would bring imprisonment or maybe death . . . and the other, the dead body he had left cold, with neck squeezed and chest caved in, wouldn't he come back for him? Wouldn't he come to separate him from her, put himself between the two of them, diminish their kisses and overrun their bed of love? These fears grew and grew with his agitation, giving him fever.

To calm down he contemplated her. Yes, she was very beautiful, and above all, he loved her. Did he love her? Did he truly feel this love, now that there was a dead man between them? No; he looked at her with fear, he stared at her small hands, and for all that he wished to avoid it, he had the feeling that these were the strong ones, the ones that had gripped his, forcing him to press. And those lips? Hadn't the death sentence for the unfortunate man come from them?

Fury rose up in him as the rebellion began, the rebellion of the decent man who feels he has been toyed with, mocked, spurred on by a force a thousand times superior; within him there rose up a hatred for her sex, an impotent rage against the weak animal capable of anything, that from the start of the centuries to their end has tethered down man, the male, the master, making him impotent, drawing his energy from him with a smile, with no effort possible to avoid it.

Her graces that had driven him mad now seemed to him ruses; her caresses, hugs of a serpent that curled around him, winding with flattery in order to squeeze and kill.

He felt an immoderate temptation to strike her, to rattle that body of such softness and beauty, asleep with a smile; he would beat her until she grew tired, until he disfigured her, in the wish to avenge himself, to avenge the strangled man, to avenge all the wretched ones whom woman had ruined ever since the serpent tempted her, ever since Jesus Christ, feeling himself a man, perhaps feeling hatred toward her sex like a simple mortal, had delivered his anathema: *Woman, what have I to do with thee?*

She woke, looked at him with her big eyes and said: "You still aren't asleep? Come, get closer to me, then you'll be able to rest."

The light of day was beginning to break and he felt dispirited, vanquished; decidedly she was a strange flower with a maddening perfume, but it was impossible to struggle; her perfume attracted so it might lull to sleep and intoxicate; this crime would be followed by another, and still others, without the specters of night, or the terrors, or what cried out within him able to prevent it; he would spend nights of fever and horror right there by her side, and would feel a desire to flee very far away from her, but all of it would be useless; a word, a look, would stop him and send him yet again to the slaughterhouse, to the abyss, to who knows where else?

Days later, when Eva de **** found out that the elated man who had spent a few days with her, now immensely dejected, now loving to the point of madness, had been arrested on suspicion of a crime, she felt something very strange that until then she had never known before. Holding back her tears, which came from unknown regions, she went to her mirror, and like those immense lethal plants that grow by some streams, looked at her reflection, perhaps admiring her beauty, unaware of all the dangers, lusts and sins that issued from her; she was like the plant that admires itself in the stream, contemplates its flower and leans coquettishly into a gust of wind, not suspecting that the wind caressing her will come away poisoned by mere contact, poisoned and poisoning.

Victim perhaps of this unknown curse, she remained in ignorance, and felt only a little love, a little tenderness for the one whom without intending it, almost unconscious of it, she had ruined forever . . . and without knowing why, she cried.

KILLER?

for Ciro B. Ceballos

S ILVESTRE ABAD, the killer, described some of his feats to friends. His blood-shot eyes took on various expressions in accordance with his narration. Here I'll tell you what, in an agitated voice, he said:

There was just one time, just once, that I enjoyed killing . . . and it was so rapid, so quick, that sometimes I think I dreamed it. I was very young then and had never killed. I had been wandering in search of work for many days, begging for a piece of bread, dragging myself along soaked by rain, scorched by sun, dead from fatigue and carrying in my soul one of those rages that inspire the temptation to destroy everything one sees and stab all those passing. I was walking along, thinking about the blackness of my luck and how unfortunate I was; and how ugly, with a gruesome ugliness that ever since I was young, people have pointed out laughing, using it to scare children by threatening them with my presence. A woman? I didn't know what that could be; they've never wanted me even for money; I make them feel disgust, I repel them, and they've always rejected me no matter the place.

That day it was already late. The countryside spread out around me, huge, immense, full of trees, plants and ears of corn, exuberant with life, proclaiming abundance and richness. I was dying of hunger.

I don't remember what happened exactly, or where I went next. Yes, I think I walked for a long time and then I stopped, worn out, on a street in a town where everyone was asleep.

A narrow street, silent, lit by a lamp hanging from a cable. I felt tired, so very tired, and also hungry; I came up to the street lamp and waited there for the first person to come along, to kill him and take his money to buy something to eat.

Nobody passed, everything was silent and I didn't have the strength to take a step. Leaning against the wall, I looked at the restless flame of the street lamp and murmured a thousand curses to myself. Others had houses, good meals, warmth on cold nights; others had family, a wife, children. I hadn't eaten in three days; I had neither mother, nor siblings, nor a friend in this world. Whenever I came to a town, dogs threw themselves on me to bite me, and children fled. I was lacking in everything, I'd never known a pleasure and my hands had never touched a beautiful object.

From who knows where, the music of a piano came to me, which I listened to with absorption, as I'd listened when I was a boy, during the short time I had a mother, to the organ of the church when the Host was raised up. I listened, I listened with delight . . . just think how beautiful it must be at night to have a woman who *makes music* while one rests in a good armchair, sheltered from the cold! And I kept listening and thinking about a thousand things, forgetting my hunger and my criminal desires.

A door opened and I saw a small form emerge. When it came closer I recognized it to be a girl; she carried a basket in her hands and moved slowly, without fear, an innocent free of any notion of danger.

The light of the street lamp fell upon her neck, a small neck that was very white, very soft and very slender. I'd never had in my hands one of those *darlings* who were the delight of others, the lucky, the blessed in this world.

My feet carried me toward her instinctively. She turned her face and I wanted to smile, but when I smile it creates a grimace that makes my ugliness more repugnant. I understood this, but despite my efforts I couldn't move away. I felt the desire to touch her, to feel the touch of her little arms, to hold her for a moment as if she were mine, and I picked her up in my arms; she wanted to shout, but distress blocked her cry. I brought her closer to the street lamp. How beautiful and white she was, white like light, like flowers! She had golden hair and a hint of a smile, just like the smile of the angels must be! In her terror she was beautiful, and her big eyes, wide-open, looked at me with dread; then I brought her toward my lips, the stiff dirty tips of my beard cutting into her face, and she shouted at the same time as she kicked my belly with her feet.

I would have to leave her, leave her and be sad as never before!

I have never been able to caress a child! I was going to leave her, but the light of the street lamp shone fully upon her slender white neck; and then I experienced the desire to squeeze it, to touch it and make contact once again with her soft skin. Since then I've felt many desires, I've wanted to seize control of something a thousand times; but never has this temptation been as strong, as urgent, as irresistible, as on that day. Not able to restrain myself, I gave in and caressed her, feeling a strange pleasure as I passed my rough calloused hand several times over her little neck, as smooth as a glove. She was mute from fright, her little eyes opened wider and wider, and she looked at me, increasingly terrified; but I couldn't, it was impossible for me to resolve to leave her, and I continued to brush my hand against her skin, over and over. Then I pressed down a little, not trying to do any harm, just to better feel in my hands this hot softness I'd never known. I pressed down and slackened, experiencing an unutterable pleasure as my fingers sunk into flesh.

Little by little, I began to press down more strongly . . . more strongly, and the flesh began to grow harder; but always, beneath my fingers, there was something as soft as velvet, which left me in raptures.

The music stopped; I heard the sound of a door opening and I felt afraid; or rather, I felt sorry that I would have to leave the girl. That little white neck! That softness beneath my fingers! That pleasure! I'd have to leave them to flee, to continue making my way, to beg and receive nothing . . . and yet even while thinking this, I continued to press down and press down on the skin, and to feel against my chest the violent beating of her heart . . . The steps kept approaching. They were coming now to interrupt me, to shut me away forever in a prison so I'd never again be able to feel this pleasure! My coarse hands would never again recreate this contact with a smooth, soft body!

I kept pressing down with anxiety, wanting, as I squeezed for the last time, to enjoy all the delight I'd have been able to feel squeezing many . . . I felt her muscles, a hardness, and then, when the steps were very close to me, I pressed down with all my strength, desiring to feel her last palpitation, her final shudder, desiring to rip her away from the others who'd be able to enjoy her while I would never, ever be able even to caress her!

And I felt that last shudder, I felt it run through her entire body at the same time as her heart ceased its beating; her neck was like a rag, it grew cold . . . a hand grabbed me but with a quick blow I rejected it, breaking away to toss the girl away and flee.

Today I still feel pleasure when I dream and believe I am pressing, pressing down and slackening. It's been the only delight of my entire life! When I see a child, I feel the impulse to throw myself on him, to steal him so I may always carry him with me, to press down on his neck and sink in my fingers. If it happened that at the same time he was carrying a glass to his lips, what great delight it would be . . . to press down! . . . to sink in my fingers! to feel that whiteness tremble . . . to shake it back and forth with shudders as small as the unmoving body, my fingers always, always squeezing!

WHITE AND RED

ALFONSO CASTRO wrote for the last time in prison. Here is the interesting manuscript:

From the reddish lips of a man of the law, a nobody with vulgar gaze and unkempt beard, slowly and heavily, my death sentence has come.

At other moments, when illness or ennui kept me in bed, I spent periods of time asking myself what my end would be; my eyes would open with all the discernment it was possible for me to give them, wishing to break through the impenetrable, to scan for and catch some glimpse of the decisive moment the future had reserved for me. The two deaths I saw as most probable were either a stupidly sought duel, or a bullet lodged in my brain by my own hand. Justice, more cautious and doubtful perhaps of my good aim, has come to save me from the job: instead of one bullet, there will be five.

During the trial—noisy and crowded as no premiere night has ever been—I hardly tried to defend myself. I heard others bellow and clamor for revenge in the name of society and in *her* name; my lawyer, whom I hardly know, a public defender, did his utmost to prove my madness or at least attribute my act to a moment of mental derangement. I believe that faced with the unforeseen circumstances of my case, the doctors would have easily declared in my favor, for effectively, in the conscience of these people, one needs to be hopelessly mad to commit a crime like mine. The members of my jury were astonished when with great pompousness in his words and an excess of black and red, the agent of the public prosecutor painted the false sufferings of the victim and the monstrousness of my feelings. This jury included the owners of a sweet shop and a grocery store, along with a distinguished moneylender; to be judged by such types has been one of the ironies, and not a minor one, in my life.

When madness was spoken of and my ancestors were paraded, invoked by the nasal voice of the defender, I got up to protest, repeating to them that my reason, as completely lucid as their own, had been particularly sound at the moment of the crime. "Given that I'm not trying to excuse myself," I added, "and have fully confessed to my crime and its motives, it seems hopeless for me to wish to make use of small-minded subterfuges. If I deserve a sentence, then pronounce it; I'm waiting for it, now that I have achieved my objective."

To pass for a vulgar killer or madman was the only thing that stirred me to rebellion, and the only charge from which I attempted to defend myself. My lawyer, who couldn't understand that the accused would not lend himself to his own salvation, didn't know what to think of me. During the hearing, when he saw my *sang froid* branded as cynicism by journalists, and when he experienced my small, or rather non-existent, efforts to help him, he took me to be a perfect idiot; alone with me in my cell, when he heard me reason about and discuss my case, he took me for sane. Why decide?

Now, what neither judges nor lawyers have understood, what in their profound ignorance of the human being and its aberrations they have been unable to fathom and instead attribute to an excess of perversity, sentencing my end as if I were a dangerous animal, is what I wish to elucidate, to explain, analyzing the causes that contributed to it, given that today erroneous human justice has no further need to intervene in my affairs.

Evidently I am not a madman! I think, reason and act like the majority of mortals, very often better. I am an ill man, I do not deny it, an ill man, yes, but a man who is ill from refinement, one who thirsts for new sensations.

When I think of my crime, I see there was no choice but to reach this point; I was predestined, marked out to follow this route, not in the same conditions as many others, perhaps, but more clearly. To recite all the crises, all the transformations of the soul through which I have passed, would be tedious; but certain events, a few accidents of life, come involuntarily to my memory.

I was born restless, alarmingly so: eager to see everything, know everything and sate myself with everything. I grew up alone, surrendering to the fantasies of my whims; in my first years this led me to reading, to which I yielded with gluttony. I devoured pages, filling my brain with opposing ideas, true or false, reasonable or absurd, permitting such contrary ambrosias to meld as they liked within me. My greatest pleasure, however, came from the strange books, the perverse ones, the books that disturbed me and that, by freezing my heart and withering my sentiments, gratified my imagination, awakening my senses to pleasures that were rarely natural; my spirit, left at complete liberty, without a fixed idea of what could serve as a norm and stimulus for existence, without a conviction to encourage it, never knew where to go, wandering constantly and shifting my thoughts at the first impression. In reality, there was never any energy or will in me; there was nothing but impressions.

When I came to understand this, I attempted to look for them, to find them in any place, at any price, as the morphine addict looks for morphine and the drunkard alcohol. This was my vice and my pleasure.

Naturally, it grew more and more difficult to take pleasure in my choices, and increasingly I had to search out unusual impressions. After months of uncontrollable orgy, in fevers of pleasure, months during which I consumed myself in the riskiest and most idiotic madnesses, there followed weeks of complete moderation and repose; I fled from my comrades in excess and moral depression arrived, which at the peak of my deliriums and eternal scavenging for sensations, hurled me toward the base of an image, making me kill the days listening to the pealing of bells, groans of organs or murmurs of prayers. But I had such bad luck that always, at the moment I most seriously hoped to believe and embark on the path toward happiness, a ridiculous phrase heard in a sermon, the hypocritical and brutally coarse face of a lay sister, or the artistic flaws of a painting would push me out, launching me once again on a search for *something else*.

My imagination could never be still. It came and went, talking nonsense, forever seeking out novelties, untiring. There were amorous whims, without love . . . moments of ardor I sought to create, whose small flame I worked uselessly to ignite. The coldness of my heart was remarkable; I didn't feel affection for anything or anyone. I would become worked up and attempt to love with madness, to feel sweep over my face something of the divine breath that made the deeply impassioned so happy . . . but I could never feel. After a month, I could only remember with effort the women to whom I'd sworn eternal love, and could never miss for more than half an hour the ones whom I had briefly embraced.

I wanted to take refuge in art, to study and quiver before the great works of the imagination, to feel the creative convulsions of the poet, musician or painter; but incapable of sustained work, I went from painting to music, from music to sculpture and from sculpture to poetry, without managing to shackle my attentions or dominate the lassitude that always quickly wound around me in inescapable spirals.

I was also ambitious and somewhat knowledgeable, having studied the great masters in depth, and the comparison between them and my own efforts made me feel disgust toward myself.

To put it briefly, I wandered amongst everything that might produce an impression on me, managing only to excite my senses and make them more subtle.

Women couldn't put up with me for longer than three days owing to my demands, and friends, with the exception of a few as sick as I was, fled from me, afraid of being swept into the whirlwind of dangerous extravagances that rose at my step.

The famous killers, the horrifying beings, the *diabólicos*, seduced me. I dreamed of characters like those of Poe, or those of Barbey d'Aurevilly; I went into ecstasies over the stories of this master, especially the one in which a couple argues and throws themselves at each other, slapping each other with the just torn-out, still-bleeding heart of their son; I dreamed of the demoniacal beings Baudelaire would have been able to create; I looked for complicated characters like some in Bourget, and for refined ones like those in D'Annunzio.

In such a state, nervous and excitable as never before, one day in a meadow I saw a certain tall, slim woman for the first time. She had a very languid walk and the pale color of a daisy. In her eyes there was something intensely dominating, with the power to envelop and subjugate. I attempted to meet her and strike up a friendship, which wasn't very difficult for me. I spoke to her, and came to interest myself in her as I'd never been interested before then in any woman. In her and everything surrounding her there was something very strange, very mysterious, which I couldn't explain or understand, and which terrified me at the same time as it attracted me; she was the only person before whom I felt myself tremble;

the anguish, the crushed sensation I felt when her eyes fixed themselves on me isn't comparable to anything. Her voice agitated me and drew me from myself; it had unique, indefinable tones, and at times—she was also a worshipper of Baudelaire—when she read out the verses of this most disturbing of poets, I felt there pass through my body something like an icy breeze. There is a stanza at the end of the sonnet "Le Revenant" that I'll never be able to forget, and that will forever coldly echo, chanting:

> *El comme d'autres par la tendresse*
> *sur ta vie et sur ta jeunesse*
> *moi je veux regner par l'effroi.*

I keep the sound and expression of these lines so close that when the bullets rip through my body, they will override the clamor of the detonation, shouting to impose themselves and truly *reigning through terror* at the solemn moment.

His house was in complete harmony with her; no sound could be heard, the slightest murmur was soon extinguished, thick carpets hushed the shuffle of steps and the doors that never creaked. Rare objects surrounded her: beautifully bound books; Russian icons with the vestments forged in metal; paintings that were medieval, or rather of the most complete modernism; masterful copies of Böcklin and Burne-Jones, and a few by Dante Rossetti; and vases everywhere made of enamel or featuring contorted Bacchantes sculpted in the roundness of the marble. All of this formed a harmony spectacularly broken by macabre figures in relief, fiery dragons, nightmarish expressions, tragic gestures in marble or grimacing Japanese masks.

Next to the piano covered in a rich gold-embroidered tapestry, beneath a terracotta bust of the monarch of Bayreuth, were all the works of this god of the Ideal Theater: the fugitive *Lohengrin*, the wandering *Tannhäuser*, the liberating *Valkyries*, the ironic *Meistersinger*, the idyllic saga of *Tristan and Isolde*, the darkness of *Twilight of the Gods* and the splendor of *The Rhinegold*.

The nationality of my so original friend was perfectly unknown to me; and despite my clever questions, I never managed to discover it; she avoided answering, but I ventured suppositions. She spoke correctly in Spanish, without any accent; she sang in German and Italian like a Florentine or daughter of

Hanover; her favorite language was French and her figure lent itself to all surmises. Sometimes I believed her to be Hungarian, other times Polish or Slavic. She obviously wasn't French or German. To be born in the Republic, the empire of contemporary art, she lacked wit and loquacity, and she was missing the stamp that distinguishes the Frenchwoman and makes her entirely personal, unable to hide herself; while to be German she lacked the heavy, slightly rude gestures, exclusive smiles, turns of speech and smiles that characterize the blonde daughters of the Rhine. And so I didn't know what to think: Italian? She wasn't that either, as she was lacking the liveliness, the fire in her eyes, movements and expression, and the heat in her voice; and Austrians are a mixture of Germans and French, with too little grace to be Parisians and too much delicacy to be Berliners or Hanoverians or Hamburgers, since German women are the same everywhere. Unable to come to any clear conclusions, I resigned myself and remained in ignorance.

One day, after Wagner's music had crashed down upon us, harsh, suggestive and torturous, she stretched out on a divan, exhausted and languid as never before. Her arms, pale as the moon, had some long red bows tied over them, which, after looping around the wrists, fell away like two wide threads of blood.

All at once, a fantastic idea took hold of my mind; I saw this white, naked woman stretched out on the same divan; I saw her, flexible, picturesque, sculpted, a hymn to form; I saw her slowly, very slowly going pale, the fire of her gaze flickering in her eyes, and the idea of my crime was born.

That night I couldn't rid myself of it for a moment. I didn't think of the consequences, which in any case wouldn't have stopped me, and I'd completely forgotten the word "crime". For me this was nothing but a supreme pleasure, an exquisite gift of a kind I'd never given myself before. She appeared to me in the darkness, persistent, ineffaceable, white, naked, flexible, a hymn to form; over the Greek island of her body I saw the bluish lines of her veins, and at the very end of them a wide thread, a red stream, a red that grew ever more vivid, ever more cruel, as the paleness of her flesh grew ever more faint, more gentle.

Now fixed upon the idea of carrying out my desire, I initiated her in the pleasures of ether. I saw how cadaverous she looked, and felt her body grow volatilized, immensely light, with no more than a small reflection of life inside it that took shelter in the brain, illuminating thought, making it see all things and discern connections with a great superiority, giving it clairvoyance.

One afternoon, as she slept without feeling she was a human creature, overwhelmed by deep sleep and wandering about some artificial Paradise, my scalpel swiftly tore through her wrists and made her blood flow, staining the clothes I clumsily pulled from her before laying her completely naked on the divan.

Blood spurted in palpitations, flowed in threads that soaked the hand and dripped from her five fingers as from five wounds, quick and almost black.

I watched her empty out, the veins growing lighter in color as their carmine abandoned them; her lips in particular turned livid as her blood continued to spill and unfurl like a tapestry. She grew pale, pale as I had dreamed, with the flight of red as gradual and gentle as it was cruel.

She opened her eyes and a convulsion went through her body; she looked at me and

then it was as if a light went out, and her palpitations of blood ended.

Her eyes fixed on mine, and her white lips
seemed to say for the last time:

> *Sur ta vie et sur ta jeunesse,*
> *moi je veux regner par l'effroi.*

And I stayed unmoving, in ecstasy before
that pallor, before that symphony in White
and Red.

WON CAUSE

for José Ferrel

THE accused remained entirely calm. Simple people found in this a proof of his innocence; members of the jury saw the attitude of an accomplished criminal.

The case fostered that novelettish interest in murders whose origin is love. The gallery was almost full and the debates had lasted for days, without arriving at any clear or definitive conclusions.

The public prosecutor's turn came. A thickset, red-faced man who sweated at all times, he filled the hall with his loud declamatory tones. He reenacted events, gloomily painted the darkness of the story, and attracted sympathies toward the victim and hatred toward the accused.

"A young man," he said, "who at the age for noble ambitions and beautiful ideals buries a dagger in the chest of a beloved woman cannot live at the heart of educated society; the spirit rebels when it thinks of the future of this thousand-times-vile soul. If at twenty-four years old he kills his beloved, what will he not do, what will he not be capable of, in a few years' time, gentlemen of the jury?"

Here the speaker pulled out a big red handkerchief, which he used to wipe his forehead and mop his neck. As soon as he'd put it away, new drops of sweat appeared. He remained silent for a moment, looking intensely toward the dock, and then his strong voice continued:

"Look at him! Beneath that humble appearance, that mask of sweetness, that almost immature face, exists a dangerous man; not a man, for he doesn't merit such a name, but rather a beast without feelings, without noble ideas, without a heart, one whom human law cannot admit. Reproduce in your memories the scene on the night of January 20th; think of that young twenty-year-old woman working to feed her sick mother, murdered out of cowardice, dragged away and thrown in a filthy sewer; justice could not act before, since the proofs were lacking, the facts grew entangled and shadow covered the deed; now light has been shed, witnesses have illuminated everything and the proofs are clear. Gentlemen of the jury," he added, raising his voice, "in the name of society, in the name of the victim, I ask you for justice. By wiping this man from the register of human beings, you will save many lives threatened by the black instincts of the one before you, already aged and advanced on the sinister path of crime!"

The counsel for the defense rose. He was a thin, pale young man, and his troubled voice echoed through all the corners of the hall. "Could the members of the jury condemn a man, a young man who in the past was held up as marked for a respectable future, when the proofs are so scarce? The accused has always observed good habits, according to his superiors and colleagues; he was an active, intelligent worker in his profession as a woodworker; somewhat violent, it is true; but wasn't that violence in many cases the proof of his dignity? His colleagues loved him, his superiors appreciated him. One day in his calm life he crossed paths with a woman, and from then on he suffered. His colleagues saw him being good to her. One night, on the outskirts of town, a bloody dagger appeared and marks in the sand were found, indicating a body dragged toward a canal. The beloved of the accused goes missing, police investigations get underway and the woodworker is arrested. But the corpse is looked for without success, proofs are lacking and justice is obliged to let him go. If he were guilty, gentlemen of the jury, once free he would have saved himself; but no, he returned to his work and has continued in the esteem of his superiors."

The public prosecutor asked to speak, and, addressing the defender, interrogated him:

"How then do you explain the disappearance of Consuelo García?"

"Very simply," replied the defense, with composure. "Consuelo was known throughout the entire neighborhood and had many suitors thanks to her beauty. Although she was officially the beloved of my client, no one except him was unaware of how lavish her favors were; at twenty years old she had already enjoyed three lovers and shamelessly passed from hand to hand, deceiving the man who felt nothing but tenderness for her. There are two probabilities: either she has fled with one of her temporary lovers—for what proof is there that the corpse thrown there is hers?—or, if she truly was stabbed, why by the man you have in front of you rather than any other of the many anonymous figures who appeared, one after another, every day? You will say there is a witness. Teófilo Cáceres, his enemy, as some have declared, with whom he spoke the least out of all his colleagues, comes along one day and swears to have seen and heard the accused and his so-called victim quarrel. He tells us that the former, in a frenzy, brought her toward the outskirts; a frenzied man, gentlemen of the jury, a man deceived in what he loves, wounds immediately, in the very place where he finds himself, without waiting for his rage to pass. And will you, gentlemen of the jury, condemn a man on the sole testimony of his enemy? Wouldn't the idea of having condemned an innocent man later be a constant regret for you? Isn't it preferable to pardon a criminal than to condemn an innocent? Pardon is noble, gentlemen of the jury, and if the accused is truly a criminal, then you will have time to condemn him later; but death is final, and if you spill his blood, whom will it weigh upon if he is innocent?"

The prosecutor replied, and since there was a point of doubt, the victim's mother was called.

She was an old woman, very poorly dressed; since an item of her statement had been requested, she repeated in full everything she had already said.

Gutiérrez, the accused, had maintained relations with her daughter for eight months before the crime; they'd seemed to love each other. Gutiérrez had treated her well, appeared to have good intentions, and even gave all his savings to her, the mother, to keep until the day of the wedding. Her daughter went away often, which led to scenes between the couple. Early that day, on January 20th, they'd gone out together, since Gutiérrez lived in the same neighborhood; at about seven at night, he had come back alone, asking for Consuelo, who according to what he had said, had parted with him moments after having gone out. "The hours kept passing. Consuelo didn't appear and I began to look out for her, as I'd expected her toward early morning. Unable to take it anymore, I went to Gutiérrez's room to let him know she hadn't come back. He looked surprised and went to look for her, returning two hours later empty-handed. I went to the police station and found that they'd discovered a dagger, which I didn't recognize. They arrested Gutiérrez, and a few months later he returned. He looked very pale and for a few days was ill."

The public prosecutor spoke again to remind them of the statement by Cáceres that he had seen them quarreling an hour before the accused returned to his house. New investigations in the canal had produced a broken skull, now present before them.

The defense, with more energy than before, maintained his client's innocence, evoking memories of innocents convicted due to the statements of their enemies. He moved the audience and members of the jury, gaining a great deal of ground in their disposition.

The accused remained completely calm. After paying attention for a long time to the discussions, he lowered his head, seeming not to hear anything further.

He was a short, slim young man, with rather long hair and a small well-cared-for mustache. His appearance was pleasant, he had refined manners and he looked somewhat nervous.

He couldn't listen to any more. The sight of the skull placed on the judge's bench, as well as the presence of the mother of his beloved, had intimately disturbed him, and in his memory he replayed the entire drama.

His fault had been to love her so much. Consuelo had dominated him completely, and despite her previous offenses, he had been prepared to make her his wife. But she took pleasure in quarreling with him, upsetting him, infuriating him, flirting with others right in front of him, and she grew happy when she saw him go pale with rage.

Ah! it was so difficult to hide his inner struggles that the jury was astonished by his calm. He had suffered cruelly in prison just remembering her, and she had risen up before him night after night, a constant nightmare! He didn't know how he'd been able to live until now, carrying the weight of this dead woman within him; because, yes, he was the criminal, and he had buried the dagger in her once, twice, three times. How had it happened? Why? He couldn't clearly explain it.

In the days leading up to it, she'd exasperated him more than usual, smiling at those who came near; he, feeling jealous, had bought the dagger, meant not for her but for one of them, the ones who had stolen her. That day, when they had gone out, she'd begun to reproach him and invent falsehoods, making him answer with violence.

At that moment they were passing near the canal, and night was falling. She, unafraid of how deserted and dark everything was, said to him, staring into his eyes:

"I swear to you that tonight I'm going with Juan. I'm off to look for him now." And she took three steps.

Blind with rage, he reached her and abruptly made her turn around. Standing before her, he cried out:

"If you take one more step, I'll strangle you, I'll . . ." She just laughed, laughed with her most arrogant, most insulting laugh, and he, still holding back, added:

"I order you not to move. I order you, do you hear?"

For her entire answer, Consuelo turned her back on him. He took her by the hair, and without knowing how, from God knows from where, he drew strength and courage: he hit her with all his strength, with all his soul! He stopped at once when he saw her fall, and contemplated her there, stretched out, more beautiful than ever before.

All his love rose up then against the murder. He kneeled by her side, he touched her heart hoping to feel something . . . it failed to beat . . . he approached her lips . . . her breathing was gone . . . desperate, he shook her, and she seemed a sack. He gave her his breath, he called to her with the sweetest names, but she didn't respond, she was dead. Thinking he would never see her again, would never hold her again in his arms, he felt something rise up to his stunned head, something scorching. Oh! The dreadful scene! Covering her with kisses, he had raped her!

The booming voice of the public defender reached him . . . the proofs were not sufficient . . . the accused was innocent . . . a few whispers said that the case had been won.

Won? That is, the criminal would be free again. Once more he'd have to return to work, feign tranquility, occasionally laugh, and always, at all times, at every moment, have to bear in his soul that horrible stain. Yet again his nights would grow agitated and fever would devour him, and in his nightmares, his horrendous nightmares, he'd still believe himself to be embracing and covering in kisses that cold, cold, cold body.

He was innocent! He was going to see the light of day, the light that warms and revives, and he would be alone on earth, since all he'd loved was dead, and he had been its killer!

Free! Was it truly freedom he was going to enjoy? Wasn't the most cruel of torments the one he was carrying within himself? Life? What interest would it have for him, if every sweet moment was interrupted by her corpse? She had been so beautiful, he could have been so happy!

And this yellow skull that seemed to fix the two hollows of its eyes on him was her, all that remained of her! He'd buried her, dragging her along like a bundle, and now this had risen up, her skull, a new motive for nightmare. Why live? Could he ever take a step on earth without regret?

Applause broke out in the hall; the public defender, exhausted, received the acclaim with pride; the members of the jury spoke to one another in whispers; the accused raised his head, but the sight of the skull, the yellowish skull, horrified him.

The cause was won.

"Accused," said the presiding juror, staring at him from behind the gleam of his lenses, "do you have anything to add?"

The accused stood up. He was exaggeratedly pale; he seemed like another man. With his gaze fixed on the skull, he said:

"Gentlemen, I am guilty of the crime. I killed her . . . I killed her . . . You must kill me . . ."

And he collapsed onto the bench.

A strange murmur echoed through the hall. The members of the jury looked at one another, surprised. The accused was disturbed. The public prosecutor had triumphed.

In view of this new statement, the trial was adjourned for another hearing. The accused went out surrounded by police officers, and as he left, he thought:

"I, perhaps, wouldn't have had the strength to kill myself."

WHY?

for Alberto Jiménez

THE letter said:

I've laughed at, I've described with far from honorable names, I've ridiculed all those who have killed themselves, and yet today, my old friend, in a few moments, you will come to spread a permanent mantle over the bed of your companion through childhood, anxieties and travels.

Why? The truth is that I don't know what to tell you, but many times I have asked myself the same question in reverse: Why live?

Do you know anything more futile, more useless, more empty and more miserly than these days which are forever tedious in the same way, to which we cling despite it all and despite ourselves, as to the most glorious and most exquisite of dreams?

I, as you have witnessed through my many and frequent crises, never found an aim in life, and in good faith, it wasn't because I stopped looking for one. For all that I meditated, for all that I tried to convince myself and imagine strengths and merits I am perfectly incapable of possessing, I have always found that everything a man can accomplish, no matter how great, is but infinitely small, without object and without duration. Accustomed to the idea that I was of no true use to others, I thought of how best to spend the days I was destined to number. I looked for intellectual pleasures, and found only hesitation, anguish and torture, in no way equivalent to my periods of healthy pleasure; the excesses damaged my character, senses and well-being; my travels gave me the impression of human idiocy seen in different climates, wrapped in fabrics more or less thick, speaking languages more or less coarse, and generally distinguishing, opining and worrying over the same nonsense. Paintings, sculptures and a few pages of a very small number of books were the only things I could find interesting in the various countries through which we passed together in our eagerness for novelty.

Back here again, I looked like one of the many who live comfortably, keep a couple of horses, change suits three times a day and lose a few bills at the club. I was a *simpático*, a pleasant young man, neither ugly nor handsome, polite and with a little learning, speaking occasionally with better judgment than the rest about the latest novel by Bourget or the most recent Parisian scandal. When I tired of the brainless marmosets who make up our elegant society, I would go to some of the cheap bars of the second order frequented by future writers, young men taken up with aesthetic rivalries, perfectly happy drinking beer and launching caustic epithets at the old men and poets who sing to the sound of the public administration's pesos. They addressed me familiarly as "tú" and received me warmly, because for them my presence was a night they could drink without paying; and since I was always informed about the poet at whom threw stones, as well as the one they praised, they were never too bored with my company, and carried on their diatribes and insults against the bourgeoisie the more loudly as more coins left my pockets.

Well then, after a short time in these boisterous and laughing surroundings, I myself would grow weary, just as I grew weary amidst the phrases and foolishness of old Rendón or elegant Gutierritos; I would walk through the streets fed up with the faces that were always the same, cursing without even knowing what it was that I so loathed, profoundly bad-tempered, feeling irritated with the old beggar women and barrel organs that abused my ears; I would enter my house to throw myself in bed, leaf through a book and fall asleep repudiating everything, including myself.

Sometimes, when my day was very black, with the hope of being like the others, amusing myself like the others, laughing at myself like the others, I would go to one of my companions from the club. "Are you happy?" I would ask, and he, with the most comic seriousness, would say: "Happy? Why yes, my good man, why ever not? Last night I won two thousand pesos at Baccarat", or else: "Happy? Impossible not to be. Would you know, I have just come from visiting the X family. Well, as I'm sure you can imagine, there were cutting remarks about the entire world, and that Olympia, now isn't she a wit! You ought to have come! How you would have laughed", or else: "Happy? Damn right I am. My mare has won first prize. Ah, how furious that made Rendón!"

I would move away with the most profound of disillusionments, convinced that neither winning at Baccarat, nor hearing Olympia's critiques, nor obtaining every first prize would bring me the slightest content.

I shut myself away sometimes, telling myself that I would do something, anything; I sent for clay and got to work on a figure, having always had a predilection for sculpting; within a few days, after having smoked several dozen cigarettes and changed twenty models, I sent statue, studio and sculpture to the devil, and more bored than ever, returned to my previous boredom.

I thought of getting married, of winning the love of a young lady and spending periods with her in agreeable conversation, attempting to divine the mysteries of the soul of a woman in formation. I don't know if it was misfortune or poor choice; the case is that all those with whom I had dealings seemed equally stupid and utterly devoid of interest. An intrigue with a married woman seduced me somewhat, but the role of a Don Juan was never for me. What's more, I feared, if not the spouses, then indeed ridicule; for every Othello, how many George Dandins exist!

All my friends were in agreement that what was lacking was a passion. I thought like them, but therein lay the great difficulty: how the blazes to achieve this passion?

I enjoyed several lovers, but ay! my friend, I was left equally disgusted with all of them. She who did not try to rob me would shamelessly cheat on me with cynicism; after a handful of such experiences, I preferred to live alone rather than so unpleasantly accompanied, even if boredom were to finish me off.

A few months after this, I met Carmen. You know the degree to which this poor woman fell in love with me; if anyone was able to offer true proofs of love, beyond a doubt it was her. All I've done to her, all the ways I've offended her, all my whims, she has tolerated; on her lips there is always the same smile, the same word of affection, and throughout my long and unbearable periods in a dark mood, no one has been as prudent as her. If I rejected her from my side, she withdrew submissively, to return after a while with words to dismantle my anger; if I was sad, her arms encircled my neck in an attempt to make me laugh, and she shed plentiful tears when she did not achieve it.

She came to domesticate me, and at times even became necessary to me, something that until then hadn't occurred to me with anyone; in short, she was so good, so loving, that I resolved to love her.

I resolved to love her, yes! To reciprocate, even if only in part, this immense affection which undoubtedly I did not deserve, which I had done nothing, absolutely nothing, to merit.

I resolved to feel affection for her; but here, my friend, the grave problem began. All my efforts were in vain; I felt nothing, absolutely nothing. I would attempt to imagine infidelities on her part, and if she went out for a moment, immediately I would concoct a story; if she arrived somewhat late, I would make myself believe I saw traces of deceit on her face; I came to convince myself of these things, but without feeling any alteration, as if she were a being who had nothing to do with me, and whom I was seeing at that moment for the first time.

In the street, amidst friends, I did all I could to miss her for a moment . . . Impossible! To think of her, I had to make an effort, for her image never came to me spontaneously. I was harsh to her, I treated her badly, I forced her to leave my home with the hope I would feel remorse, long to see her, experience anything that would speak to her presence within me . . . For the eight days she didn't live with me, I felt her absence only in material things, as if she were a maid to whose service I had grown accustomed, and when she returned with tears in her eyes, swearing she couldn't live without me, I could barely feel a little pity, and at the same time envy, yes, a great envy for being able to love like this.

I reached the point of attempting to turn to the comic, telling her she'd deceived me or begging a friend to seduce her, in order to stir something within me. Only the fear of ridicule could stop me.

At the same time, I held the strange conviction that in not loving this woman, I was incapable of loving any other. I already knew, and to my misfortune very well indeed, the cruel ones, the ones who play with sentiments, the ones who had attempted to exasperate me and nearly deceived me in my presence. Since none of them had made me feel either, what was I to think?

Slowly the idea began to form within me that I did not have a heart, that it was withered and dead. I turned my gaze toward the past, looking for some affection without being able to find it.

You know very well what my childhood was like. Of my father, I have no memory; of my mother I remember a being totally absorbed in herself, with a severe face that intimidated with neither a caress nor a kind word ever coming from her mouth. I do not doubt she loved me, no, but she loved in her own way, that is to say, in a way completely opposed to mine. Everything in me was effusive; I was an explosive little child, either joyful to delirium or devastated to despair. As a boy, my mother daunted me, and once a man, I grew used to seeing her as a separate being, in whom I could trust nothing nor ask for anything. I went my way, and when she died, I made an effort to cry for her, thinking that perhaps she had suffered, that in the depths of her soul she had some secret pain hidden away of the kind that erases the smile from one's lips forever. I had no friends, I fell in love with no one, and I continued to live without loving and without being loved.

The entrance of this woman into my life, with her caresses impossible for me to return with honesty and sincerity, have convinced me that the source of sentiment in me is exhausted. If I had seen affection around me, if tender words had been spoken, then perhaps I would have been otherwise. Evidently, as in all men, I possess the vibrating fiber that reaches out, and is attracted to other fibers in sympathy; but these were not encouraged and had no help in their development. Now I am incapable of crying over the misfortunes of my peers or myself, am barred from ever giving a rich kiss from the soul and am obliged to tell lies at every moment, which bring unhappiness to the one with the tragedy of loving me.

My situation is clearly as follows: I cannot love. Crippled and poor of heart, the pleasures of the sentiments were not made for me.

In such a state, condemned forever not to know affection, what can I hope for in life? Evidently nothing, as the proof is that I desire, desire with all my strength, to love the being *whom I feel that I would love if I were able to love*, but I cannot! I cannot!

After meditating a great deal, I have resolved to kill myself. The best thing, perhaps the only good thing possible in life, isn't it love? I am incapable of feeling it; if the sole sweet thing is hopelessly closed off to me, what use is existence?

I cannot even love myself, feel for my own being and whims anything more than I can feel for others! No, not even the good fortune of being an egoist has fallen to me.

I have gone to her bed and kissed her, with the hope that having decided to die, I would feel something upon leaving her forever . . . I felt nothing. She opened her eyes, looked at me with her usual tenderness and drew me to her breast . . . I stood up feeling lost, asking myself what fatal destiny, what punishment weighs upon me that shuts me out forever from the paradise of tenderness; and with a loaded pistol by my side, remembering those whom I have ridiculed, I write this letter to you.

Tomorrow they will laugh at me as I have laughed at others, yet who has ever lived without knowing something of the worm, the leprosy, that gnaws into the souls of suicides?

A HYPOCHONDRIAC

for Federico Gamboa

"OH, NO! Obviously she will not catch me, it's impossible. I know her habits, her tricks and ambushes.

"I feel her when she approaches, when she touches some object, when she roams about pursuing me, coming ever closer. It hasn't been easy work, but I've managed to outsmart her. No, I will not let death take me by surprise!"

With shining and dilated eyes, shallow breath, and a deep confident voice, thus spoke the madman to whom I had been led. After a brief pause, he continued:

"For you see, Death, sovereign Death, immensely powerful, one and multiple, present, making her rule felt at all hours in all places—Death, shadow of God unfurling like an immense flag, lording over the world, over beings and objects, surrounding everything, lying in wait for everything, closing it within a circle ever more narrow; Death, she who alone truly exists, would never, ever snatch away men if they took the trouble to study her.

"She can never arrive when one expects her, when one is prepared. It is possible to flee from her, ah! The great scoundrel! No one is so malevolent and so great a liar as she is! But me, me, she will never deceive me."

A cold laugh followed his words, and his eyes, the horrible eyes of a madman, dilated further, taking on a dark expression.

From the depths of my heart there rose up a great compassion, at the same time as an immense fear, a terror.

He had thought, behaved, understood, felt and loved like us, but one day the terror of death had entered his soul, to leave only with his reason. I understood how easy it would be to be carried away by this very madness, one day, one night, with a glimpse of this threatening lady.

I knew his story; I had been his friend and attended to him in his hours of deaf anguish, from the moment the obsession with death had entered into him.

Ever since then, he had seen her, felt her, found her in all places; sometimes, desperate that he would be unable to live without constant nightmare, he called her name and attempted to stop her in her path. Many times I found him stretched out on a divan, body unmoving and eyes closed, waiting for her, wanting to *let himself be surprised*.

Nothing was more horrible than his nights without sleep and without peace. If for a moment sleep calmed him, very soon he would wake up terrified, in a cold sweat, his heart beating intensely, believing his final moment had come, opening his eyes as wide as he could to see objects for the last time and touch the heart he thought was going to stop forever, with the anguished horror of death in his soul.

After some time, his thought held only one idea: Death, dominating and invincible Death! I'd seen him cry with impotence, in the belief that he was hopelessly condemned, and unable to do anything, alter anything or speak a word to anyone.

If he was walking in the street, he would study all passers-by and devour them with his gaze. Sometimes a rage, a nervous agitation, made him shiver with envy.

They would live. They would continue to enjoy the sunsets, the radiant afternoons, the brilliant moonlit nights, everything he so loved; *they* would love, and vibrate with a thousand pleasures, while he, their equal, just as strong and healthy as they were, would sleep, lost and forgotten in the mansion of eternal darkness.

There was no repose for him. The awful image appeared everywhere. A beautiful woman with flushed cheeks, everything that spoke of life, only made him see skeletons—and perhaps his only consolation was to imagine all those he saw as dead.

"Just think," he said to me sometimes, "it is impossible, completely impossible, to escape her. Think of how my life with its desires, my body that beats and moves, will tomorrow, in a month, perhaps two, be gone"—and he closed his eyes to sample the torture of seeing nothing. "What will I be, what? Motionless, dead, unfeeling as this table."

Other times he would lie down in his bed, wanting to imagine death; but if there was the slightest complication to his circulation, if he felt some manifestation of the physical, he would jump up, go to the mirror, and look at his face as if wishing to convince himself he was still alive, even as at every moment he waited to collapse.

The only thing that calmed him was to walk, walk with urgency, thinking of *her* in his dread and trusting he could escape her.

The sight of a funeral procession or a cemetery would drive him out of his wits. He would feel the temptation to run away or hide himself, like a coward before a superior enemy.

His days went by like this, in constant desolation and eternal terror. Every morning he was surprised to find himself alive, every night he went to sleep with the fear of never rising again.

In the end, in a dark and terrible mood, almost desperate, when he felt he was truly dying, madness arrived as a Redeemer. By carrying away his reason, it also carried away his terror, because from that day forth he has believed he will be able to avoid her, has believed he will be able to flee from her and dominate her by his wits; and he is happy.

As I moved away from my old friend, I tried to peer into the greatest depths of my own thoughts, wanting to know if there was a seed of his terror and madness. It would be so easy!

And as I walked through the long corridors, and saw many others who with our limited scope we judge to be miserable, I remembered the old torture of my friend and his current tranquility, and said to myself:

"Perhaps the happiness that we seek so desperately exists only here, in this sad home, in these poor unbalanced brains, in these beings alive because of a chimera, a lie, madness in short."

THE RIGHT TO LIFE

for Balbino Dávalos

WHEN she abruptly announced her condition to me, my throat felt as if it were being crushed, and my tongue curled up refusing to articulate the words that threatened to flood out like a torrent.

Pregnant! A child! For me these two words represented something absurd, strange and solemnly ludicrous that had never passed through my imagination in the time I had lived by her side. A child!

For the whole day these three syllables did turns in my head, without my being able to force them out. They seemed to be three insects, three pests that with their constant flying had come to batter the walls of my brain.

Then I doubted, for it was obvious she had made a mistake; my reason said it couldn't be, but why couldn't it be? I myself didn't know, but *it couldn't be*. Maybe she wanted it, or expected it, hence the reason for her self-deception.

At night I questioned her, and she said:

"Yes, I'm sure now, I feel it. Just you wait and see, he'll be adorable and take your name."

Her words did me harm. They rang out, they struck me with a hammer's blow . . . She was sure now, she felt it! . . .

Her stomach went about deforming and slowly took on a repulsive roundness. The perfect lines of her hips slumped, her walk became awkward and small yellow spots covered her skin. Although I tried to hide it, I felt disgust and rage; for me this deformity was a desecration of nature and an attempt against the beauty of the body that had seduced me, which I had loved only for the harmony of its forms.

She felt anticipated tenderness for this creature that slowly took shape in her womb, a womb now deprived of all charm since it was not barren; she caressed her belly, imagining she was caressing her child, and in conversation spoke only of him, exciting the irritability that had taken control of me since the arrival of this being no one had called. The creature altered and upset our peace, and robbed from me some of the affection to which I had formerly laid sole and absolute claim.

I also felt compassion and pity for the one who was going to arrive without asking for it, the one who without realizing it, not knowing how, would fall into an existence of which he remained unaware. For my entire life, and also owing perhaps to how unexpected she herself had been, I have resolved never to have a child, never to reproduce in an heir all the seeds of misfortune, disgrace or corruption I might harbor. During my years of youth, the trials, the harshnesses, the deceptions were so great that more than once I reproached the memory of my parents for having thrown me into a vain struggle, as undoubtedly I had been born for a different life. In my blackest hours, with my spirit in turmoil and my stomach crying out in hunger, how I envied those who did not exist! All the tortures I saw around me, the abandoned children, the lepers, the criminals, awoke in me an infinite sadness. I wanted to go and embrace them as brothers, saying to them: "You, poor abandoned ones, you must curse the memory of the one who, unaware of what he was doing, sent you here to disown you! You must show him your stinging sores, your infested fistulae, your body corrupted by evil; you, who are perhaps totally ignorant, came to this world without knowing how and killed without knowing why. And yet, if the most secret fibers of each being were revealed, anyone might have turned out to be a killer." My reasoning could appear monstrous now, but I believed it to be very logical.

I had periods, during my years of blackness, when I fled from woman, and hated her for having received the mission of conceiving.

Around me I saw beds of prostitutes, as well as beds authorized by a representative of God, where such work—a work of desolation and tears—was carried out each day with the greatest simplicity, as if flinging out wretches this way to yoke to life's heavy cart, as if spreading such misery and pain, were the most lawful and honest thing in the world.

I came to fear, as if they were dangerous beasts, the ensnaring gaze, the joining of mouths, the throbbing of thoughts in unison, because from the brilliance of these gazes, the moistness of these lips, the communion of these thoughts, emerged the stunted or lush plant that the sun would burn, the cold would freeze, the rain would lash, deprivation would pursue! From a few words of love exchanged, from a fleeting union organized in the dark of night, an existence likewise full of darkness would be born, and more than one kiss has been responsible for many crimes.

In my conscience, I had thus come to formulate the principle clearly and precisely. To irresponsibly cast into life something that feels and understands nothing was just as ignominious and cruel as the torture of an innocent.

He was born. The sketch of a child twisted in the bed, his little throat burst out in shouts and his half-open eyes barely shed tears, as if even the light made him suffer. I looked at him with an irritated expression, feeling nothing but contempt for myself.

This was me, this was her, this was both of us together in what had emerged from our affection and caresses. Me and her, in this howling little animal that tore open its lungs to scream, perhaps as a protest against us. I saw him grow; I saw him with his mother and myself dead, miserable and ill-treated by the existence to which he'd arrived crying; I saw his fists, clenched just as when he was born, rising up toward the sky, his heart bleeding, his lips mouthing a curse! I saw him suffering in many other ways, while she, broken and still in shock, wept in our stained bed. Regret hounded me . . .

The bedroom was almost entirely dark. His mother slept deeply, as I, sitting in my chair, meditated in the shadows.

From my egoism, from my actions looking for nothing but pleasure, the consequence was *him*; the consequence would also be his good or bad years, undoubtedly dulled eventually by sorrow. I was the one responsible for all he would commit in life; I had indirectly put the rifle into his hand with which in the name of country he would kill his brothers; I was the one responsible if, inheriting my profound disgust for everything, he picked up a homicidal bomb that attracted people's revenge against him; I was the guilty one if bequeathing to him my sensibilities, he poisoned his years through the impulses of the heart; I was the one responsible for his acts, the one to whom he could ask:

"With what right, on whose order, did you rip me from the nothingness in which I was sunk? Why did you drag me from the profound darkness and absolute ignorance in which I found myself? Was it to bring me to a place of delights, rewards and peace, where good brothers can be found who help each other, where a caress does not hide a claw, where the thought you have given me does not torment, and where it is possible to live without worries? No, isn't that right? Then what for? What is the aim of your work?"

And these words, echoing like an accusatory cry, disturbed me. In the shadows a man seemed to be gesticulating, my son; he seemed to be looking at me with eyes of rage, eyes in which I read all the regrets, anxieties and sins that I myself bear.

Then I went to the bed where my accomplice was sleeping; through the glass of the window I could see the stars with their cold shining gaze. I contemplated my child, thinking of the wandering nights that perhaps awaited him, and the moment his eyes would turn uselessly toward the indifferent darkness of this sky. In my mind one idea remained, unswerving: the idea that as soon as possible, at the very first opportunity, I would liberate my son by taking away his life.

RAY OF MOONLIGHT

for Baron Salvador de Maillefert

I am in a hospital for the mentally ill. My entire symptom, my entire madness was to state what I have seen, and insist upon it.

Nobody is as aware as I am of the bizarre and unbelievable nature of my account; I myself have doubted, and have believed myself to be the plaything of hallucinations. But always, after many doubts, I have come to the same conclusion: my story is true, terribly true, and she has left me with an impression of terror prepared to awaken at any moment. The silent and melancholy night, the night in which I previously liked to feel myself alone and awake as the rest slept, the ministering night full of silent murmurs and gentle charms, this night once beloved is now hateful to me.

Every sound, every movement, the running of a rat, the wingbeat of a fly, a door creaking, a breath of wind, the painful or desperate cries of madmen, everything startles me and fills me with anguish, because I believe that *she* is returning.

How much time has passed? I don't know, and who will ever know? I know nothing, I can explain nothing except that this has happened and has left an unforgettable impression on me that likely will drive me to madness.

It was night, in December. I had worked for many hours, and at last gave in to exhaustion. Everything was in silence, a silence of the tomb; everything was dark, a darkness of death, and only the yellowish light of my small lamp made the paper gleam. To one side, the clock ticked, marking out the march of time and filling me with joy. Within me everything was also calm; only my heart, the beats of my heart, responded like an echo to the *tick-tock* of the little machine.

I left my desk to get into bed, and when I turned out the lamp, everything went black. I closed my eyes, hoping to sleep. One hour, two hours went by like this in silence and darkness. A suffocating heat devoured me, and opening my eyes, I looked for the light . . . Everything was black, everything dark.

Lying still, I began to think. The darkness, the night, the silence, everything unsettled and perturbed me for reasons I did not know. A stupid terror of the mysterious took hold of me: silence, night, darkness, were they not death? Was I alive?

Did movement, light, men exist? Or was I living alone in a dream? I laughed at my own foolish questions, and listened . . . Nothing, complete silence. I concentrated my attention even more, hoping to surprise a faraway murmur, the wingbeat of a fly, the *tick-tock* of my clock . . . but the same silence continued, and no sound came to me. I thought of universal death and the ruin of the world, and believed myself to be alone, terribly alone. Then I hoped to listen to the beating of my heart . . . There was nothing there, either. All was silent, all was asleep. My solitude was complete.

My anguish kept growing when the moon came out and her pale, calm, translucent light filled the room. The most brilliant rays fell onto a large red quilt that I had let fall in my sleep. Spread out, it looked as if it were receiving the dream of this luminous lady, many centuries old.

Through the window I saw thousands of glittering stars let their ash of gold fall to earth, where the snow shone like an immense cloak of silver. On the prickly dry branches of trees, something was draped like immense transparent boas. I felt happy, I contemplated the face of the moon for a long time, I traveled through the stars and newly in love with night, I returned to tranquility.

Or rather, not tranquility, because I don't know the influence that beautiful nights work on me. They completely change me; I feel my body grow lighter, my intelligence more alert, and my senses and desires more awake, along with my childish curiosities.

What beings might dwell in those stars, which for us are beautiful fires made to illuminate nights of love? Could they have poets there, could they sing stories, could they be happy? How much I thought, looking at those lights which attracted me, and how great a desire I felt to go outside, breathe in the perfumed air, sink my feet into snow, and walk for many hours as I'd done at other times, with my gaze fixed on the stars, my mood calm and my mind awake, feeling the desire to love and love, under the radiant clarity of the moon.

Then, ah! What happened then, how to describe it, how to express what I felt, the fright it gave me to hear a very slow, very drawn-out, very long sigh? If I hadn't been in my bed, surely I would have collapsed, so deeply did it shake me and make me tremble; but my fright and anguish were even greater when, upon turning my face—I don't know how I had the courage—I saw there, stretched out on the red quilt, a white shape, the shape of a woman bathed in rays of moonlight.

After the first fright, I thought my eyes had played a trick on me, and I looked back toward the ground with attention . . . but no, they hadn't deceived me! A woman dressed in white, her hair loose, seemed to be sleeping. I could see the unhurried movement of her chest perfectly well, and the sound of her gentle, calm breathing came to my ears.

I stayed there unmoving, on the bed—I don't know how I was able to sit up—leaning on an arm and looking, looking motionless with terror; looking without thinking of anything, almost unconscious, so overwhelmed was I by what was happening; looking at that white figure, the figure of a woman silhouetted against the red of the quilt, which had sunk under the weight of her body.

Then she gave a drawn-out, very long, very pained sigh, longer, ah! yes! than the first. The sigh sent through my entire body, through my bones, through my blood, through my skin, something I can't define, something, oh God! which didn't kill me for reasons I am still unable to comprehend.

The woman had opened her eyes and looked at me intensely, although with indifference. She seemed to see, but not to look. In her expression there was sadness, a great sadness, and she was pale, as pale as I must have been. Her eyes stared into mine as our gazes met, hers tranquil, mine . . . I don't know, nor will I ever be able to know what mine was like! Ah! Who can express the horrible difficulty in breathing I felt at that moment? Who can understand the terror produced by the fixed gaze of a being—was it a being?—what was she, what was she, oh God! . . . I intended to speak, to address a word to her, to question her perhaps, but from my mouth only a few almost imperceptible sounds emerged.

She sighed again with greater sorrow than before. Each sigh was more and more drawn out—for me, each sigh lasted an eternity.

How long were we there, she with eyes fixed on me in an ineffable expression, and I watching her, motionless, unable to speak? For me these were many years of suffering;

my heart beat violently and afterward seemed dead; I felt a terrible cold, and sweat ran down my face.

Then the light that bathed her disappeared, and all was left in darkness, including her. I didn't see her but felt her, and sensed her reclining at my feet, looking at me with her big eyes, exaggeratedly wide-open.

She stood up. I felt her; I saw her white cloak go to the window. Then there was nothing, only silence, darkness and terror, a great terror in my soul.

Without knowing by what impulse, I jumped out of bed and shouted with all my strength, with my previously dead strength, so that everyone in the house crowded in, looking at me with astonishment.

I went over the entire house and closely examined my window, located at a great height. Everything, everything was closed; nobody could have come inside, nobody, nobody, nobody!

All night long I waited, full of impatience and terror, not wanting to go back to my room. I waited, pacing from one side to another and containing my heart with my hands so that it didn't jump; because it hurt, it knocked against me as if wanting to burst out. Oh! The terrible night, the long night, immense and eternal!

At last day arrived, which I had awaited as one does salvation; with it tranquility came to me. I thought it had been a dream, a hallucination, and I went back to my room.

The first thing that leaped to my eyes was the spread out red quilt . . . the red quilt that still showed signs of the body that had reclined on it, bathed in the rays of moonlight.

I could take no more; letting out a cry, I lost consciousness.

Then they brought me to this home, this home for madmen, but I am not one. With my own eyes, I have seen her big eyes fixed on me; I have heard her long drawn-out sighs of sorrow. I am not mad, no . . . and to think that the woman might come to this home!

I am not mad, no . . . The night is hateful to me. When I see it, I tremble . . . and she might come back here, perhaps with the return of the moon.

WHAT THE BEGGAR SAID

for Alonso Fernández

IT had been three years since I'd last seen him, and that night, when he stretched out a skinny hand to me that I remembered as muscular and strong, I was taken aback. The truth is that he'd become someone else. Everything had changed about him, his manners, the features of his face, even his voice. His beard, previously very neatly groomed, now grew in disorder, gray and without any elegance. His eyes appeared agitated, suggesting long periods without sleep, and there was something profoundly devastated in them that especially intrigued me. In vain I tormented my memory trying to recall some accident, some unhappy event that had taken place in his life and troubled him in some way.

No rumor had come my way. I knew perfectly well that he wasn't married, that he didn't have family and that he hadn't known any passion. What could it be?

A short time afterward, when he'd gone away, I said to my neighbor:

"Franco has changed so much. When I knew him, he was so different!"

"Yes," he replied, "everyone has noticed the change. I believe that he's somewhat disturbed. All of a sudden he stopped being what he was, stopped seeing his closest friends, let himself go. Now there you have him, always silent and sad like he's in the clouds, only rarely going out."

"Some misfortune must have come to him, some death, something, in short, to explain it . . ."

"Not as far as I know, at least. His change was abrupt, overnight, and no one can find out the reason. Maybe he has some secret."

The conversation was interrupted by the arrival of a few other gentlemen; the meeting took on interest, the conversation became general, and yet I, with my curiosity now awakened, couldn't stop thinking about my friend, making surmises and concocting fantasies about the reasons for his odd attitude. Keeping an eye on him, I saw him in the background talking, or rather giving simple answers, to a lady who was quite beautiful and not totally shy, according to what was said.

Previously, when I'd known him, he'd distinguished himself for his chivalry with the ladies, at times exaggerated. Gallant to excess, he had owed several enviable conquests to his tact; he gave compliments, was not averse to spending lavishly, and always and in all circumstances was the first one prepared to commit the greatest acts of madness, if there was a chance they might win him a special look or smile. Now his manners were very different; tired, as if distracted, he gave his answers without paying attention, indifferent to the conversation. A few moments later he was left alone, a vague shine still in his eyes, and I, no longer able to hold back, approached him.

We spoke of insignificant things, of the people gathered there, and then, without warning, when I least expected it, he questioned me.

"A short while ago you published some studies about the supernatural, isn't that right?"

"Yes," I answered, looking deeply into his eyes, "everything out of our reach and our perception attracts me, especially the unknown forces that surround us, guide us and perhaps motivate us without our suspecting them. Unfortunately, we have nothing precise, nothing conclusive at hand. Who knows if there is really nothing, and all we imagine are mere stories we compose to give ourselves a fright? It wouldn't be strange if once a man is dead, nothing survives of him."

My interlocutor didn't answer, but shook his head to deny this, and after a long pause in which we both remained silent, as if hesitating and still undecided, he murmured:

"I know something . . . something that . . . might help you in your investigations, something"—and as if he suddenly found the courage, he went on with energy—"something, anyhow, that I don't know how to describe, but that has happened to me, something I cannot doubt, that simply *was*, *was* undeniably, and that torments me. Listen to me, and do not believe I am raving.

"It was the Tuesday of a carnival that I had spent happily in the company of friends, all of them young and quick to enthusiasm. At some moment well into the night, when the dance had begun to take on more liveliness, I began to feel irritated and worried for no reason. My unease increased so much that attributing it to the warm atmosphere, I decided to get some air, and so I put on my coat and hat and went out into the street.

"After a few steps I was ready to go back, but some instinctive force stopped me. I felt repugnance for the place, for the groups of lascivious dancers, for the tables where a woman in a domino mask drowned herself in champagne and babbled obscenities that excited people and made them laugh. With a vague sadness, a presentiment of something I couldn't quite put my finger on, I lit a cigar and headed for home.

"I walked slowly, drinking in the night air, looking at the empty streets, thinking of the sleep that had resisted me for days. Few things at the time were as tedious to me as going to my room and finding myself completely alone; to feel distant from every human being filled me sometimes with a fear at which I would later smile. My room was hateful to me, yes, because there was nothing in it that gave it life and nothing that attracted me to it. That night, to kill time, I walked around the streets at random, feeling sad in my solitude. I looked at the clouds, at the sky full of stars, and thought of our poverty, of how infinitely small we are. In this way, philosophizing with the seriousness of one who leaves a place of pleasure where he has grown bored, without quite knowing how, I fell to thinking about death.

"Tired out, I turned on my steps with the intention of going home at last. When I reached the corner of my street, I ran into a beggar whom I often gave alms. I hadn't seen him for some time, and his presence at that hour and that moment didn't fail to vex me somewhat; but kind to the unfortunate out of principle, hospitable because nothing makes it impossible that someday we'll find ourselves in their situation, good with an egotistical goodness, if you like, nothing but a hope of being treated the same way in the same conditions, I spoke to him.

"'Have you been ill, old man? It's been so long since I last saw you.'

"He only made a movement of his head that meant nothing, and when I raised a hand to my pocket to give him something, he grabbed my arm, paralyzing all movement. The hand, his hand which I felt in its coldness through my clothes, had a metallic rigidity; astonished and even somewhat alarmed, I looked at him, but his face escaped me in the darkness of night. With a peculiar shiver, I heard his voice:

"'Ah, señor! Thank you . . . I have come from so far away!'

"With my astonishment increasing, afraid of the unusual tone of his voice, I answered:

"'Well then? You don't need anything from me, my old man? Where have you come from?'

"'Ah, señor! I've come from so far away . . . from there, on the outskirts of the city. I've come from the cemetery.'

"'From the cemetery, at this time? You are mad!'

"'Mad? I thought so too, but no; I'm in my right mind, or I was . . . I don't know if I am, or I was.'

"For me it was obvious that he was indeed mad, and since we would have gone on like this until my door, I said goodbye to him, holding out a coin.

"'No,' he said to me, 'don't go in yet. I want to tell you . . . Do you want to know?'

"'What is it? It's late and I'm sleepy. Better wait for another day.'

"I was about to leave, but *something, something* stopped me, stronger and more powerful than my will. Was it perhaps the old beggar's especially peculiar voice? Was it his mysterious accent? I don't know, but I stayed there without moving, leaning against the wooden door.

"'Yes, I have come from the cemetery, but not from above. I have come from below, from the land where they buried me. Do not laugh; I have died, I died the day after you gave me alms for the last time. I had an attack, I felt something had grown paralyzed inside me, I couldn't move and they buried me, they buried me, yes. Ah! Good señor! They say the holes where the dead stretch out are black and cold. I don't know, I felt nothing and the only thing I did was reason, eternally reason. Hunger? Heat? None of that is known there; the body feels completely well, but here'— and he pointed to his head—'here everything moves and does turns.

"'Imagine a man who has the most powerful, most intense of memories; that was me. I saw myself as small, I saw all my actions, my movements and even my words. Yes, I heard even the most insignificant of words there inside. Then, who knows how much time later, I saw myself as a boy, and all my pranks, all my little perversions, returned to me with incredible precision; only now, I commented on these deeds and words. I thought of how in such circumstances I should have worked to behave well; I repented for having done certain things instead of others; I despaired for not having done them. Up to this point, it was almost bearable; but then came the age of maturity, of the great perversions, and everything I had missed, everything that tortured me for not having acted in this or that manner, in this or that circumstance, cannot be described. I saw myself as loved, rich, powerful and calm, and saw perfectly the causes of my guilt, the reasons why such a fortune had not come to be. I saw myself begging, and if I did not feel the nauseas of hunger and cold, I did feel the bitterness of the insults received. If on earth I had asked myself why I found myself in this state, there in death I knew, and knew I alone was the guilty one. When the moment of my death arrived, I returned again to my first years, and then the ideas and reproaches repeated. Like this, once, a hundred times, it was always the same, always a reliving of my existence and always a vision of how it should have been. Ah, señor! There is no comparable torment! Ah, señor! A thousand times hunger, a thousand times rain or a night without shelter than this constant reasoning and constant thinking; having done this instead of that, I would have had this which is good rather than that which is bad.

"'I could take no more! When the moment of my death arrived and it began again, I don't what happened to me.

"'Death is horrible, señor. Think of an artist, a painter who exhibits his picture or an author who sees the curtain rise on his piece, who then abruptly has a clear intuition of its defects and a clairvoyance which makes him see this same work as perfect, while being unable, irredeemably unable, to correct it. The same thing happens with our lives, there in the other region.

"'Death is horrible, yes! How deceitful and contemptible are those who make us believe in rewards and pleasures, how deceitful also are those who say there is nothing. There is, señor, there is, and not even the most holy one will remain in peace, because who has never made a mistake in this world? What saint has not committed errors and continued down one path rather than another? When seeing that another road was traced for him, when seeing how sterile and vain his toils and mortifications were, his torment would perhaps be even greater than our own.

"'I, ah! I have escaped, I have overcome death! At first, unable to take any more of it, I made an effort, an effort, yes, with my entire will; an effort that lasted for a long time, a very long time, and that at last gave vigor and movement to my body, a gigantic strength to lift up the earth and escape from that hell. Hell, señor, after we die, is nothing but our own thoughts, our previous life that we see at the same time as a scene presents itself. There we find painted and described everything we have scorned, everything we have gone past without even suspecting it, everything we should have been and most ardently desire, along with the trivial reasons why we did not achieve it. Ah, señor! One feels a fury to begin life again, and there is no temptress worse than death. Our punishment and our sorrow is to feel this constant temptation!

"'I, ah! I have escaped; I have escaped from the hell of my thought. I have laughed at the tormentor, because with my will, my supreme strength of will, I have escaped from this immobility, and can now order my thoughts and tell men:

"'Good and evil, there in the distant region of death, the place where only thought lives, do not exist. Nor are there any prizes or penalties. There is nothing but temptation and reasoning about what one should have done. Those who were poor in the world will see the ways to have achieved wealth; those who suffered will see how they should have felt pleasure; those who tortured themselves, how they should have laughed; those who cried, why they did not feel delight. The thirsty will see they had water in their hand; those unlucky in love will hear the secret of being irresistible, and nobody, nobody will have peace if he hasn't known how to be happy on earth. The happy ones in this world will be the happy ones in the other. No one else!'

"The beggar was silent. I, stunned, did not know what to think. I looked at him with eyes of doubt; truly, I did not know how to react, so unexpected was the perturbing account of the old man.

"Then he opened his long overcoat, and since the moon was escaping from between the clouds at that moment, the light shone fully upon him. I could see it, I saw it . . . his worm-eaten face, fleshless in parts, his eyes dripping yellow liquid . . . I saw his chest, torn-open, with everything putrefied and dirty bones. Around them everything stirred about, decomposing and filthy. I saw . . .

"Nothing else, because that's when I fainted. I haven't seen the beggar since. What do you think of all this?"

A PARTIAL LIST OF SNUGGLY BOOKS